Marjorie Dea

Josephine Chase

Alpha Editions

This edition published in 2022

ISBN : 9789356785830

.

Design and Setting By
Alpha Editions
www.alphaedis.com
Email - info@alphaedis.com

Contents

CHAPTER I.

IN THE STUDY

The sun that pale spring afternoon had appeared only in brief, tantalizing flashes. Of a sudden it burst through the curtain of ashen gray clouds, behind which it had been hiding, into flaming glory. Its warm rays rioted down through the long windows of Brooke Hamilton's study, filling the stately room with radiant light; transfiguring the face of the single occupant.

"Oh." Marjorie Dean raised her brown eyes from the time-stained sheet of paper she had been studying. She greeted the wealth of cheerful sunburst with a fond friendly smile, blinking a little at its almost too-ardent attention. It caught her, embraced her, caressed her lovely, smiling face; splashed her bright brown curls with gold.

"You're an affectionatious old dear, even though you *did* skulk behind the clouds all morning." She made a valiant but vain effort to fix her eyes directly upon the king of day. "Can't do it. You are altogether too dazzling for me." She raised a shielding hand to her eyes. "Anyway, I'm glad you are here, full force. I saw you peeping out from behind the gray quite a while ago. I was too busy then to be sociable."

"Please, Missus Biographeress, were you talking to me?" broke in an inquiring, respectful voice. "I wasn't always like this, so I wasn't." Came an eloquent silence.

Marjorie left off trying to stare the sun out of countenance. She glanced about the study in half startled surprise. The door leading into it from the hall was closed. She suddenly laughed, a merry little gurgle. She fixed an expectant gaze on the study's back wall.

"I know where you are," she called out. "No; I wasn't talking to you. I was talking to the sun."

"Then you must be crazy." The voice was now minus respect. Instead it harbored smothered laughter.

"No, Jeremiah Macy; I am *not* crazy. But I am *very very* busy."

"That's almost as bad as being crazy," came the sympathetic opinion of the still unseen conversationalist. "I hope you're not too crazy, excuse me, busy, to deign to grant your humble friend, Jeremiah, an interview. Think of our happy bygone campus days and don't be snippy. Be not only great, Bean; be cordial."

"You win. Never dare call me snippy again. Since you are *right behind* the secret panel you may as well appear in the study." Marjorie gave laughing permission.

"Thank you. Your cordiality sounds genuine. I trust nothing has gone wrong with my hearing. Ahem. What?"

The secret panel in the back wall of the study slid noiselessly to the left; disappeared into its hidden groove. The square opening it left framed Jerry Macy's chubby, pink and white features decorated with a pleasant smile. Her head was poked forward like that of a speculative turkey. Her intensely blue eyes were trained upon Marjorie with an expression of impudent mischief.

"Here I come." She bent her back and bundled through the aperture. "Ah-h!" She straightened with satisfaction. "Always close the door after you, Jeremiah." She leaned forward; pressed the small oblong of wood which formed the hidden mechanism of the sliding panel. Next instant the opening had vanished. The high brown wainscoting again stretched unbroken along the study's rear wall.

"That secret panel is certainly a comfort to my lonely old age, Bean." Jerry cast a grateful eye in its direction. "If I had come to the door of this sacred haunt you might have chased me away. But you couldn't resist the panel method. Result—enter Jeremiah." Jerry waved a complacent hand.

"That's one version of how I happened to let you in," teased Marjorie. "Here's another. I knew you knew something new on the campus that I didn't know. So I 'deigned to grant' you an interview."

"Hm-m. You're not as noble as you might be. Never mind. We won't speak of that," Jerry hurriedly assured.

"So kind in you," Marjorie murmured, "or rather, so wise."

"Precisely my own opinion. I may achieve greatness as soon as you." Without waiting for an invitation Jerry slid into a high-backed chair exactly opposite that of Marjorie at the long library table.

"The girls will be here at five," she announced. "They're going to take us back to Wayland Hall with them. Leila has a new idea for a party. We're to stay to dinner at the Hall. Miss Susanna's resigned to it. She was invited, too, but she said she was 'no buttinski.' What do you think of that? It shows I've accomplished some good since I came to the Arms. I've taught Miss Susanna several pithy bits of slang, and Jonas is learning fast."

"I should say he was. The other day when he took me to town in the car he told a motorist, who tried to run in ahead of us to park, that he was 'too fresh' and to 'cut out his nonsense.'" Marjorie gave a reminiscent chuckle.

Jerry smiled cheerful gratification of this news. "To make use of my own pet vocabulary: It's up to me to show a hot-foot," she declared. "While I enjoy lingering in this classic spot with you, beautiful Bean, I shall not linger. You heard what I said about five o'clock. Heed my remarks. I must go now." She made a feeble pretense toward rising. She rolled humorous, entreating eyes at Marjorie.

"Oh, you may stay." Marjorie became loftily tolerant. "First you may tell me everything you know about Leila's new stunt. Afterward, I have a splendid job for you."

"I don't know a single thing about Leila's new stunt. She 'phoned me about half an hour ago and said she and Vera would come for us with the car at five. She said she had a fine idea but that we'd not hear a word about it until after dinner at Wayland Hall tonight. Anything else I might say on the subject I'd have to make up. You would not care to have your faithful Jeremiah resort to fiction, would you?"

"You're a faithful goose. I'm not so news-hungry as to ask you to desert the truth, Jeremiah," was the merry assurance. "Leila, the rascal, knows we're eager for campus news and plans. She loves to create suspense and keep it up till the very last minute. Now I'm going to set you to work. You may sort some letters for me, if you will."

"Will I? My middle name is willing!" Jerry drew her chair closer to the table with a grand flourish. A pleased light shone in her blue eyes. She was very proud of having already assisted Marjorie on several occasions in the work of arranging the data, prior to the writing of Brooke Hamilton's biography.

Readers of the four volumes comprising the "MARJORIE DEAN HIGH SCHOOL SERIES," know Marjorie Dean as a high school girl. They have learned to know her still better through the four volumes which comprise the "MARJORIE DEAN COLLEGE SERIES."

Returned to Hamilton College as a post graduate her work in connection with the building of a free dormitory for ambitious students in adverse circumstances has already been recorded in the three preceding volumes of the "MARJORIE DEAN POST GRADUATE SERIES," respectively entitled "MARJORIE DEAN, COLLEGE POST GRADUATE," "MARJORIE DEAN, MARVELOUS MANAGER" and "MARJORIE DEAN AT HAMILTON ARMS."

Because Marjorie had deeply reverenced the memory of Brooke Hamilton, the founder of Hamilton College, she had come into an intimate friendship with his great-niece, Miss Susanna Hamilton, the only living representative of the Hamilton family. For many years Miss Susanna had been at enmity with the college board. Shortly after the death of her distinguished great uncle, Brooke Hamilton, she had turned against Hamilton College and refused to furnish the data for a biography of the founder which was to have been written by the president of the college.

Due entirely to Marjorie's hopeful, sunny influence Miss Susanna had eventually emerged from the shell in which she had lived for years. She had decided that, since Marjorie had most revered the maxims and memory of her great kinsman, she was therefore the one best equipped to present him truly to the world in a biography. She had invited Marjorie to be her guest indefinitely at Hamilton Arms and had turned over to the youthful biographer the data for Brooke Hamilton's life story.

Marjorie had said good-bye regretfully to Wayland Hall, her college residence of almost five years and moved to the Arms on the first day of March. With her had gone a second cordially invited guest, Jerry Macy, her roommate and chum of Sanford high school days.

During their first week's stay at the Arms the two girls had been the center of a jolly little social whirl. Miss Susanna had insisted on entertaining their intimate friends at tea, luncheon and dinner. The festive week had ended with a reception to the dormitory girls at which the Travelers, Jerry's and Marjorie's sorority, were the guests of honor.

Then had followed Marjorie's introduction to Brooke Hamilton's study as her literary work shop. There she had been affectionately established by Miss Susanna and supplied with a cabinet full of Brooke Hamilton's personal letters and documents.

How long she might be engaged in the pleasantest task she had ever undertaken Marjorie could not say. As a labor of volition it demanded the best effort of thought and judgment that she could summon. With her usual lack of vanity she was not attaching much importance to herself as Brooke Hamilton's biographer. Her whole heart was set upon doing justice to a great American by a faithful presentation to the world of his integrity and genius.

"Do you realize, Jerry Macy, that we've been here at the Arms almost a month?" Her back to Jerry, Marjorie asked the question as she delved industriously among the packs of neatly tied letters on the top shelf of the cabinet. "Today's the twenty-fifth of March."

"I know it. How much of Brooke Hamilton's story have you written?" Jerry came back curiously.

"Not any of it as I intend it shall finally stand," Marjorie confessed. "I've made plenty of notes, but they only complicate matters at present. There is so much material, all intensely interesting. It would make a twelve volume biography. Miss Susanna wishes it to be a one volume story. My head is full of Hamilton history. It is positively maddening sometimes to try to keep track of all I read, and plan how I shall arrange it. I was never intended for a biographer, Jeremiah."

"You only think you weren't," Jerry encouraged. "After you have got away with Brooke Hamilton's history and covered your beautiful self with glory you may take up biographing as a steady job. I'll permit you to jot down the story of my life. I'll try to persuade my friends to confide their life stories to you for publication. There's old Hal, for instance. He——. Oh, forgive me, Marjorie. I didn't intend to be personal." Jerry's instant apology was regretful. "I wasn't thinking of a thing, but the funny side of Hal's having his biography written."

"Oh, never mind, Jeremiah." Marjorie was more embarrassed by Jerry's apology than she was at mention of Hal's name. Her face flushed hotly. She kept it turned toward the cabinet, rather than let Jerry see her confusion. A pause, then she added generously: "Hal is good enough to do great things in the world. Perhaps *you* may someday write his biography as that of a personage. There! Found at last." She affected deep interest in two bundles of letters which she took from the cabinet.

"No, Marvelous Manager; I can't see myself as Hal's biographer. He'd insist upon seeing every line I biographed before it was hardly off the bat. He wouldn't like a thing I said about him. If I wrote words of glorious praise, he'd say 'stuff' and 'slush.' If I failed to glorify him as a baseball artist, a promoter of yacht races and a four-time winner of the Sanford half-mile dash, he'd say I was stingy." Jerry retrieved her blunder with this humorous flow. "*No, siree.* My genius runs toward jingling, not biographing. Get that? If Hal ever longs to see the story of his life in print he'll have to get busy and write it himself."

CHAPTER II.

THE WORLD WIDE SECRET

Marjorie was laughing as she resumed her seat at the study table. She was quick to understand the purpose of Jerry's ridiculous and elaborate objections to her really sincere words concerning Hal. Her flash of self-conscious embarrassment had vanished in quick amusement of Jerry's remarks.

"These are letters to Brooke Hamilton from friends," she explained as she shoved the two packs across the table to Jerry.

"He must have been right in line for a popularity prize." Jerry eyed the tightly-bound, thick stacks of letters with comical respect.

"They represent the correspondence of only four or five men. Each letter isn't from a different person, my child," Marjorie said lightly. "Your job is to put the letters of each person in separate piles. You may have that end of the table all to yourself."

"I get you, Bean." Jerry energetically gathered up the two packs of letters and moved with them to the upper end of the table. "Watch my speed, my efficiency, my celostrous usefulness. By the way, my new word is on the gain. I've persuaded Jonas to use it, Miss Susanna thinks well of it and Leila says it is clever enough to be Irish."

"It's a good imitation. Celostrous—sounds like a real word, even though it isn't," laughingly commented Marjorie.

"Sh-h-h. Somebody might hear you." Jerry held up a cautioning finger. She cast a roguish smile toward a vividly handsome face which looked down at her from a portrait on the wall. It was the face of Brooke Hamilton. Life-size and life-like the deep blue eyes seemed almost to twinkle an answer to Jerry's mischievous smile as she continued to gaze at the portrait.

"He's so real." Marjorie turned her head over one shoulder to glance up at the pictured face of a strong man in the noon of manhood. A friendly smile played upon her lips. "I hope you haven't minded my sitting with my back to you this afternoon, Mr. Brooke," she apologized.

"If that was a magic portrait this is the way it would be. 'Then the enchanted portrait spoke from the wall and said: "Don't mention it, beautiful Bean. Go as far as you like. Even the back of your head is an inspiration to me. I can never be grateful enough to you for writing my biography. How is your friend, Miss Macy? She is a lovely girl and I—"'"

"Jeremiah, you disrespecter of great persons!" Marjorie sprang from her chair and made a frolicsome pounce upon Jerry. "Stop it this minute."

The two tussled gently for a brief instant, then fell laughingly apart. The blue eyes of the man in the portrait seemed almost to be watching the merry conflict.

"You see how utterly you disrupt serious work," Marjorie pointed out severely. "I have half a mind to take the job I gave you away from you."

"You can't. I have it cinched." Jerry snatched up the two packs of letters and tucked one under each arm. "I love the job. I'll do better, Bean. I promise on my sacred Jeremiah honor."

"I haven't the heart to take those letters away from you," Marjorie jestingly conceded.

"Glad of it. Kindly don't bother me. I am going to give a violent demonstration of the word 'work.' It's three o'clock now." Jerry peered down at the tiny open-face, necklace watch she wore about her neck on a fine-linked platinum chain.

"I knew it was nearly three. I've learned to tell time by the sun since I came to the Arms and began my work here." There was no timepiece in the study, nor would Marjorie wear a watch when she came into it to work. She did not wish to reckon her daily faithful application to the biography by time. She liked to lose herself in the thought that all time was hers in which to do Brooke Hamilton's memory honor.

Jerry followed her announcement of industry by a business-like attack upon one of the packs of letters. Soon she was deep in carrying out Marjorie's directions. Marjorie resumed a reading of the paper in which she had been engrossed when Jerry had entered. It was a dissertation on democracy in Brooke Hamilton's fine, clear hand.

Silence took up its reign in the study. Marjorie was deep in the dissertation. Oblivious to all else Jerry interestedly sorted letters, reading pertinent snatches of them. Neither saw the sliding panel in the back wall of the study begin to move slowly. Neither saw Miss Susanna's head appear in the opened square.

For fully a minute the old lady watched the industrious pair with brooding, tender eyes. She had thought Marjorie alone in the study and had come to her by the secret entrance in the same spirit of play which had prompted Jerry to use the sliding panel. In one hand were three letters for Marjorie which Jonas had just brought from the mail box at the main gates of the Arms.

As soundlessly as she had appeared in the secret doorway the visitant disappeared. In noiseless obedience to her touch the panel slid once more into place. Miss Susanna trotted down the long hall and on down the wide staircase. Her small face was illumined by a bright smile. She looked as though she had suddenly discovered the world-sought secret of happiness.

She continued on out the massive front door, down the steps and across the lawn to where Jonas was clipping long sprays of furry pussy willows for the two tall Chinese vases at each end of the sitting room mantel.

"You ought to see them, Jonas," she burst out happily. "They're both in the study, lost to the world among Uncle Brooke's papers. I came away without their knowing I saw them. I couldn't bear to disturb his helpers, Jonas. And I once thought no one but the president of Hamilton College was fitted to write his biography!"

"Strange things happen, Miss Susanna." Jonas's silver head wagged itself solemnly over the huge bunch of pussy willows he was holding. "He'd be better pleased, though, to have things as they are now. I believe he'd rather the little girl would write his story."

Jonas invariably spoke of Brooke Hamilton as one alive, but traveling in a far country, rather than of a man who had passed from earth.

"I think so, too, Jonas." The instant, eager response brought a pleased gleam to the old man's eyes. "He founded Hamilton College for the higher education of girls. It seems as though Hamilton has at last shown appreciation of him by raising up a student after his own heart. That student is Marjorie Dean." She paused, apparently taken with her own fancy. She added sturdily: "All the more reason why she should be the one to write his biography."

CHAPTER III.

TWO HAUNTING BLUE EYES

"Hurray for Wayland Hall!" Jerry sketched a lively step in front of the dressing table mirror as she gave her reflection a last fleeting glance. "The Arms is a magnificent, palatial roost, but where, oh, where, are our little pals?"

"At Wayland Hall. Sometimes I wonder if you might not be happier there with the girls than here with me." Marjorie brought a half wistful look to bear upon Jerry. She stood gazing at her chum, a lovely contemplative study in black and white. The straight cut of her white corduroy gown with its wide rolling collar and deep cuffs of black satin was so simple as to be exceptionally effective.

"Want me to shake you until your curls bob straight off your head and your teeth clatter like castanets," Jerry growled menacingly. She made a threatening advance upon Marjorie, her blue eyes set in a determined stare.

"No, indeed." Marjorie promptly put a high-backed chair between herself and Jerry. "I'll protect my coiffure to the last gasp. I took pains to put those curls precisely where I wanted them to be."

"Then don't make any more foolish remarks, Bean." Jerry halted. The set expression of her eyes changed to one of dancing fun. "I'll set you a good example by not making any more myself that might even sound foolish. I know my own follies as well as I know yours."

Marjorie leaned her arms on the crest of the tall-backed chair. She smiled rather absently. How like Hal's eyes Jerry's were, she was thinking. Recent mention of Hal had brought him to the foreground of her mind. Now she thrust memory of him impatiently aside.

"I'll be nicer to you than you were to me," she told Jerry. "You look very celostrous, Jeremiah." "Celostrous" was a pet word of Jerry's own coining. "Your dress matches your eyes and the silver beading on it looks like fairy mist. It's a frock of frocks." Marjorie continued her admiring survey of Jerry and her becoming finery. As she had remarked the gentian blue of the crepe exactly matched her chum's eyes.

Again Hal's handsome, resolute features sprang into memory. This time memory played her an unkind trick. She saw Hal's eyes as they had appeared in that unforgettable, unguarded moment as he had paused before the portrait of herself at Castle Dean on Christmas Day.

She had then come into a very disturbing realization of how much pain she was causing him through her lack of love for him. She had tried to forget, knowing that she could offer no remedy. Work had largely driven away that disturbing memory since her return to Hamilton. Those two blue, despairing eyes returned to haunt her only upon receipt of a letter from their possessor. There had been only two letters. Marjorie had not answered either very promptly. She sometimes went so far as to feel that she might be better pleased not to hear from Hal. Still she did not wish to deny him friendship.

"You are *too sweet* for words." Jerry broke in upon her train of reflection. She purposely simpered so as to hide her pleased embarrassment of Marjorie's compliments.

"Am I?" Marjorie was not even seeing Jerry now. She was seeing Jerry's brother who refused to retire from her somber reflections. No; she valued Hal's friendship as dearly as she did Leila's, Jerry's or that of any of her chums. Her adoration was for her captain and her general only. Now that she had a clearer understanding of Hal's disappointment she felt a more personal sorrow toward him. She had glimpsed the desolation of a strong man's soul. The revelation had awakened in her a truer sympathy for him.

"Come out of it." Jerry had paused directly in front of the chair on which Marjorie was leaning her elbows. She waved her arms making vigorous passes before the day-dreamer's face. "What is the matter, Bean? Two minutes ago you were one grand sweet smile. Now your expression is werry sad. You *have not* lost your last friend, Bean. Take heart. Jeremiah is here. Ah! I have it! Nothing like Bean Jingles to put the chee in chirk. Here we go!

"Celostrous day; rip whoop-ter-ray;

We celebrate with zest:

Your feathers preen, resplendent Bean,

All dressed up in your best."

"According to your jingle 'resplendent Bean' must resemble a vain, strutting peacock." Marjorie came out of her retrospective reverie with a giggle.

"No, indeed. I never meant to suggest such a thing. Regard yourself as a bird of Paradise, dear Bean," Jerry corrected.

"I am not so conceited. Besides, I'm not dressed up in my best. This particular set of feathers is far from gorgeous; and not even my second best."

"Have a heart. Remember the claim of poetic license, and respect it. Your practical, unpoetic criticism is *so* discouraging. Don't put on the brake. There are more rhythmic inspirations to come. I feel them whirling madly in my gifted brain. I merely stopped for breath. Whir-r-r-r! Buzz-z-z-z! I'm off again.

"Oh, forth we'll hike, upon the pike,

Beyond the campus wall;

We'll tread the green, sweet, agile Bean,

Until we hit the Hall.

A charming pair, we'll mount the stair;

Dear one, then take my arm:

Safe to fifteen, bewitching Bean

I'll guide you without harm."

CHAPTER IV.

THE SPRINGTIME OF THE HEART

"And you will please trouble yourself to recite that jingle again before it vanishes into nothingness," commanded a laughing voice from the doorway of the large, old-fashioned sleeping room. Leila Harper stood in the half-opened door, an attractive figure in the newest of English leather motor coats and sports hats.

"Leila Greatheart, what a *dandy* coat and hat!" Marjorie cried. She came forward, hands outstretched to meet Leila.

"Here I come with a fine Irish dash." Leila made a funny cat-like leap into the room and caught Marjorie's welcoming hands in hers. "It is a hundred years since I saw you; or so it seems," she said in her whimsical way. "Now I shall say not a word more until I have taken down Jeremiah's jingle. I happen to have a pencil, and bewitching Bean herself will furnish her Celtic friend with a bit of paper."

"At your service. Let me conduct you to the writing desk," Marjorie took Leila's arm and escorted her to an open antique mahogany desk. She motioned Leila into the mahogany chair before it. "There you are." She indicated several sizes of pale gray note paper bearing the monogram of the Arms. "Isn't this beautiful paper, Leila?" she commented. "Miss Susanna put it here on purpose for us. She never uses it. She prefers white. This was Mr. Brooke Hamilton's own stationary."

"You are two lucky children in a fairy castle," Leila declared. "Now say me the jingle, Jeremiah. Then we will talk about everything and anything."

"Ahem." Jerry coughed importantly. "I may have to depend upon bewitching Bean to help me. I never remember my own ravings—inspirations, I should say. Inspiration is—it is—well, it just is."

"Is it?" Leila inquired with raised brows and an engaging grin.

"It certainly is," Jerry responded with a difficult solemnity. It broke up in an amused high-keyed chuckle. Merely to glance at Leila, posed in an attitude of expectant and ridiculous affability was to laugh.

After one or two hitches and a little prompting from Marjorie who also had designs on Jerry's funny effusions, Leila managed to record the three jingles, though she had arrived in time to hear only the last one of them.

"Now we have a beginning." She exhibited open satisfaction of the penciled copy of Jerry's lively doggerel. She folded it twice and placed it in a pocket of her leather motor coat. "I shall expect you to take down and save me all future jingles of Jeremiah, Beauty, since you are the inspiration. Never fail to do so. Now you may talk to me about anything. I am so gracious."

"I have copies of two jingles that Jeremiah spouted last week on an occasion when I brought her four letters from the mail-box. I'll mail you copies of them tomorrow. Where is Midget? I know she can't be far away."

Marjorie glanced inquiringly at Leila.

"She is lost somewhere in space downstairs. She is but a small doll in this great house. And you now promise me two more jingles. Two and two are four, and four is better than two. Soon we shall have a book. It must have a green crushed Levant binding with a portrait of Jeremiah reciting one of her own jingles as a frontispiece and the story of her life printed in gold letters on the front cover."

"It looks as though I might become as famous as Bean, Harper, Page or any other campus high light if that crushed Levant edition doesn't flivver," Jerry said hopefully.

Full of their usual light-hearted raillery the trio of girls presently went downstairs to find not only Vera Mason in the sitting room with Miss Hamilton. Ronny Linde, Muriel Harding, Lucy Warner and Robin Page as well were there, clustered around Miss Susanna. They greeted Jerry and Marjorie with a concerted shout and rushed them affectionately.

"How did the four of you manage to keep so quiet?" Jerry demanded. "I'm amazed."

"You needn't be. You were so noisy yourselves you didn't hear us. But *we* heard *you*," Vera assured. "We heard three different varieties of giggle, all going at once. Leila was told to hurry upstairs and bring you down instantly. Instead—" She cast an accusing glance at Leila.

"Ah, but you were in good company, so I may be forgiven." Leila made a gallant bow to Miss Susanna.

"You certainly are a fine Irish gentleman with your lordly manner and nice leather overcoat," complimented Miss Susanna, her brown eyes dancing.

"Am I not?" modestly agreed Leila. "What I need most to make me impressive is a pair of green leather boots and a chimney pot hat."

"I'll cast you as the romantic Irish hero of a play in precisely that costume. See if I don't," Robin Page laughingly threatened.

"Who will write the play?" Leila quizzed interestedly.

"You of course." Robin leveled a designating finger at Leila. "That's a bully idea; to give a romantic Irish play. And for once you may act as well as be stage manager. So glad I happened to see you this afternoon and hear about your green leather boots and chimney pot hat."

"As you will not require anything of me but to write the play, manage the stage and play the leading part I'll not change your gladness to sorrow by snubbing you. Still I am wondering where I am to find the boots and the hat. And let me add a condition of my own. I will not be stage manager, actor or playwright unless Miss Susanna will promise to come to the show." Leila launched this proviso with her most ingratiating smile in Miss Hamilton's direction.

"I'll come," the old lady obligingly promised. Now that she had "surrendered," as she humorously termed her change of heart toward Hamilton College she was almost as eager as her girls to have some part in campus fun and enterprise. "Will it be a house play?"

"No it will not." Marjorie and Robin spoke the same words, and almost together. They looked at each other and laughed. The same thought had prompted the same answer.

"Wise Page and Dean. They see money in featuring Leila as the hero in her green boots and chimney pot hat," was Ronny's light explanation of the exchange of eye messages.

"Do we? Well, *rather!*" Marjorie said with warmth.

"Uh-huh," emphasized Robin. "The campus dwellers will mob the gym to see Irish Leila as an Irish hero in an Irish play. We'll reap a bully harvest of dollars for the dormitory."

"You and Vera can do that Irish contra dance you danced at Page and Dean's first show when we were junies." Muriel grew animated. "In itself it's worth the price of admission."

"Oh, *do* have it in the play, Leila," rose the general plea.

Leila bowed, hand over her heart. "How celebrated Midget and Leila are! That means Midget must play the part of the maid from Lough Gur, of the county Limerick. That is the place in Ireland where the fairies yet hold their invisible revels. And I think Midget might be taken for one of the Lough Gur fairy queens," she said fancifully. "I am afraid to invite her home with me to Ireland for fear the fairy folk may steal her and shut her up in a mountain."

"Not if I see them first," Vera was positive upon this point.

"Midget is small, but valiant." Leila rolled laughing eyes at her friends. "Ah, but you would not *see* the fairies, Midget, when they slipped you away. You would not see them until you were safe inside the mountain."

"Then I'll keep far from Ireland. I'll be Irish in plays only," Vera vowed.

"Be sure and save a good part for Luciferous Warneriferous," was Muriel's next thoughtful request. "She simply loves to act."

"Oh, I do not." Lucy looked alarmed. A gale of laughter went up at her horrified denial. "I can't act. You know that, Muriel Harding."

"You should learn to act," Muriel said with severity. "It is your duty. *I* am giving you good advice. These persons are laughing at you."

"Who made them laugh? Keep your advice. I'm furious with *you*. Br-r-r!" Lucy shook her head savagely, thrust her chin forward and fixed her greenish eyes upon Muriel in a frozen glare which convulsed that delighted wag. She thoroughly enjoyed teasing dignified Lucy to the point of retaliating.

"Oh, splendid! You look every inch a villain!" Muriel simulated profound admiration. "You have true histrionic ability, Luciferous. Let my flattering opinion sink deep, and encourage you."

"I'll let it go in one ear and out the other," was Lucy's derisive retort. "Don't *dare* choose me even for a villager in your Irish play, Leila Harper. I'll be far more useful as a press agent. I'll get up a handbill about the play, and mimeograph it."

"Bully idea, Luciferous. Be sure and hit all the high spots. When you have the handbills ready you may stand outside Hamilton Hall and distribute them to the campus dwellers." Jerry patted Lucy on the shoulder with force.

"Ouch! That's one of my high spots you just hit." Lucy dodged out of Jerry's reach, rubbing her assaulted shoulder. "I'd rather give out handbills any time than act," she declared with a defiant glance at laughing Muriel.

"Be calm, Luciferous," soothed Leila with an assuring grin. "I would rather have the handbills than you on the stage as a villain. It is Matchless Muriel who may have the pleasure of playing that part. She will have plenty of lines to learn." Leila nodded significantly toward Muriel who merely continued to smile.

"Biographers, bill posters, stage managers, actors, et cetera; attention!" Vera called out. She pointed to the tall floor clock, imperturbably ticking off the minutes. "It's five minutes to six. Too bad I always have to be time crier for this reckless aggregation." She heaved a dismal sigh. "What *would* you do without me?"

"Be laggards all the rest of our lives, faithful Midget. You are one of the world's finest institutions." Leila beamed patronizing appreciation on her diminutive chum.

"I know my own worth. I am surprised to find you have an inkling of it," Vera retorted with complacent dignity.

"A dignified Midget is so impressive," murmured Leila. "See how wrapped up in her small self she is. She has forgotten about being town crier. I see I must—."

"Don't trouble yourself. I'm still on the job. It's now five minutes later than it was five minutes ago," Vera hastily announced.

"Come, good Travelers." Muriel took the middle of the floor in a stiff recitative attitude. Raising one arm she declaimed in a high stilted voice: "Let us journey with all speed toward shelter ere dark night o'ertakes us."

"Something like that," was Ronny's ultra modern agreement. "With so much talk and so little action it may be midnight ere we see the Hall. I'm not speaking of myself, or of Miss Susanna. We're not loquacious."

"*You* only miss being loquacious because you haven't happened to start an argument with Matchless Muriel. I should hope you *weren't* speaking of Miss Susanna." Jerry put on a shocked expression.

"Don't squabble over me," Miss Hamilton said in a meek little voice. Followed a burst of ready laughter. She said as it died out: "I'm going to send you home now, children. Come back tomorrow evening to dinner. Bring Kathie and Lillian with you. Robin, please invite Phil and Barbara. Tell Phil to bring her fiddle. I will invite Peter and Anne Graham, and Signor Baretti. He will like to come to our party. He and Peter will be company for Jonas. I shall make Jonas sit at the table with us."

The Travelers thought Miss Susanna's sisterly regard for Jonas one of her finest characteristics. While he had been a youthful servitor of the Hamiltons during Brooke Hamilton's declining years, he had filled the triple role of brother, servitor and friend to the Lady of the Arms during her long lonely reign in the great house. He was many years older than Miss Susanna, but still a strong, sturdy man.

Jonas looked upon Miss Susanna as an empress, to be reverenced and obeyed. Miss Hamilton's oft repeated assertion to him: "You are a direct importation of Providence, Jonas, willed me by Uncle Brooke," had made a deep impression on him at first utterance. As a consequence, his one aim in life was that of faithful service. Rarely could she coax him to appear socially at the Arms, even among the few friends who knew his worth.

"You're always thinking up something perfectly, splendidly hospitable!" As she rose from her chair to see the Travelers to the front door Marjorie pounced lovingly upon the Lady of the Arms, wrapping both arms around her.

"A hold up, a hold up!" cried Jerry. "I'm going to join in it." She made a playful attempt to pry Marjorie's arms loose from about the old lady. The others gathered around the pair, mischievous and laughing. They put Miss Susanna through a gentle wooling which left her with ruffled hair, her lace collar awry and her cheeks pink from the loving salutes of fresh young lips.

The Travelers went down the wide stone walk from the house looking back, waving and calling gay good-byes to the small, alert woman at the head of the veranda steps. The gate reached, Marjorie turned to wave her hand again. She mentally contrasted Miss Susanna's happy expression of the present occasion with the sharp, doubting, half resentful gaze the mistress of the Arms had turned upon her when she had first been ushered into the library by Jonas to meet Brooke Hamilton's kinswoman. Where there had once been shadow, somber silence, loneliness, was now light of love, gay friendly voices, sympathy, companionship.

It had been Miss Susanna's wish that Marjorie and Jerry should be at the Arms to greet the return of Spring. Remembering this a rare, rapturous flash of exaltation swept over Marjorie. She was thinking as she waved her hand to the little old lady on the veranda that Spring had not only returned to the Arms. It had miraculously returned to Miss Susanna's heart.

CHAPTER V.

FOR THE GOOD OF THE "DORM"

"What's on your mind, Leila Greatheart? You've thrown out tantalizing little scraps of what I'd call non-information ever since we left the Arms. Now stand, and deliver." Marjorie made her plea for enlightenment as Leila closed the door of her room and favored her chums with one of her bland, wide smiles.

Dinner over at the Hall, the eight Travelers had lingered in Miss Remson's snug office to talk to the little manager for a pleasant half hour. They had just made port in Leila's and Vera's room for what promised to be a most interesting session.

"What's on my mind, Beauty?" Leila regarded Marjorie owlishly. "More than you might think, should you judge by appearance," she said with mock seriousness. "I am enchanted with myself because of my own schemes. Sit in a circle around me and listen to the golden runes of Leila, the witch woman. I see gold, gold, gol-l-d."

She made a sudden forward sweep of the arm toward Jerry who was about to seat herself on Vera's couch beside Lucy Warner. Jerry raised a mild shriek of surprise, flopped against Lucy who was near the end of the couch. Unprepared for such a jolt, Lucy rolled off the end of the couch to the floor. Jerry clutched wildly at her arm. Her balance upset she followed Lucy to the floor and sat down upon her amid shouts of merriment from the six gleeful spectators to the double mishap.

"Now see where you put me." Jerry still sat on the floor regarding Leila with an air of deep injury. Lucy had scrambled to her feet and made for a chair. "The very least you can do is help me up. Give me your hands, and don't dare let go." Jerry held up her hands to her still mirthful hostess.

Leila essayed the task of raising Jerry to her feet. Laughter robbed her of power to lift Jerry. It also robbed Jerry of power to raise herself from the floor. After three separate attempts at co-operation, all mirthfully unsuccessful, Jerry was hoisted to her feet by the combined efforts of Marjorie, Ronny and Muriel.

"You are an awful hostess." Jerry opened her mouth widely on "awful" and ducked her head violently forward at Leila. "First you scare your guests by making wild sweeping swoops at them. Then you laugh at them when they come to grief. This time I'll choose the middle of the couch, and be safe." Very cautiously she re-seated herself on the couch, squarely in the center.

"We'll sit one on each side of you, Jeremiah, so that you can't fall off the couch again." Ronny plumped down on the couch on one side of Jerry. Muriel obligingly seated herself on the other side.

"*I* was shoved off that couch and sat upon by Jeremiah, yet no one appears to remember it," Lucy mournfully complained.

"I remember it. You tipped me off your lap," accused Jerry.

"But you tipped me off the couch first," reminded Lucy. "I forgive you, but never again will I sit on a couch beside you."

"I always try to look upon everything that happens as for the best," Jerry returned with angelic sweetness.

"There were no bones broken, but there was plenty of fuss made." Leila thus summed up the accident. "Now pay attention to me, and let us have no more nonsense." Whereupon she burst out laughing, thus starting her companions' merriment afresh.

Quiet finally restored she began again. This time with the fine earnestness which she could readily summon when occasion demanded.

"Travelers, dear," she addressed the now attentive seven, "we have left only six days of March, then April, May and the early part of June in which to earn money for the dormitory. We must give as many shows as we can manage between now and Commencement. We must give the Irish play the first week in May. I shall write it in one week. It will be nothing startling, but it will be a play, I grant you that. I shall have a sorry siege to make the cast learn their lines in two weeks. It must be done. We must rehearse four nights in a week. Vera will make cunning Irish token cards and we shall sell them for a silver quarter apiece."

"First I had heard of my new job, but I accept. May I inquire into the mystery of an Irish token card?" Vera asked with an assumption of profound respect.

"You will draw many little pictures of the cast, Midget, on many little cards," was Leila's somewhat indefinite answer. "You will learn more about my Celtic schemes when I am not so busy."

"Oh, very well. See that *you* don't interrupt any of *my* busy hours. If you see me put up a busy sign on my side of the room, respect it," warned Vera.

"See that *you* do not again interrupt *me*," flung back Leila, scowling portentously at her diminutive roommate.

Everyone else interrupted, however, and Leila had to come to a laughing stop in her harangue until she had enlightened the party regarding "Irish token cards."

Like her artist father, Vera was gifted with the ability to draw. Leila's idea of having small, head-and-shoulder, pen-and-ink sketches of the various characters in the play drawn on oblong cards, three by one and a half inches, was decidedly interesting from an artistic as well as a financial standpoint. Below the sketch would appear the stage name of the character, the true name and the date of the play.

"Vera won't be able to do many cards, Leila. She won't have time. She can't make the rough sketches until we have our costumes and know ourselves how we are going to look," was Ronny's doubtful view of the feature.

"Oh, I can draw the different characters as they ought to look. Leila can show me the style of costume to be followed by the actors. I'll draw each character once, leaving out the features till I know who will be who. Then I can fill in the blanks with the familiar eyes, noses, mouths and ears of the illustrious cast. After that it will only mean hours and hours of tedious copying my originals." Vera made a triumphant outspreading gesture of the arms indicative of her mastery of the situation.

"How we do miss Ethel Laird," sighed Ronny. "She was so clever. Do you remember how gorgeous those posters for the first show were that she painted. What became of them, Marvelous Manager?" She looked quickly toward Marjorie as though seized with a sudden idea.

"They're with the other properties in the Page and Dean section of the garret," Marjorie replied. "At least they were still there the last time I was up garret. That was after the Valentine masquerade. What is it, Ronny? I see you have something on your mind."

"Let's have an auction," eagerly proposed Ronny.

"Not now; not until the first of June. We could clear up all the stuff we have used for advertising the shows, and other treasures of our own that have campus history, and auction them off. Let Jerry be the auctioneer. Oh, lovely! What?"

"Oh, lovely," mimicked Jerry. "There is nothing very lovely about hard labor."

"No use in pretending, Jeremiah. You know you'd revel in being an auctioneer." Ronny shook her finger at Jerry.

"I've heard of worse stunts," Jerry admitted with a grin.

"I have nearly as good an opinion of you, Ronny, as I have of myself," Leila graciously conceded. "You and Jeremiah have my permission to manage the auction. You may collect all the wares for it, and do all the work. Between times, when you have little to do, you may dance in my shows."

"*Your* shows?" Ronny's eyebrows ascended to a politely satiric height.

"*My* shows," repeated Leila with great firmness. "Have you not yet learned that Page and Dean amount to little without me. It is Harper and Harper who should have all the credit."

"Right-o!" exclaimed Marjorie and Robin exactly together.

"Now why did you agree with me?" Leila demanded, her tone full of innocent Celtic surprise. "That was merely one of my Celtic jests."

"'Many a true word,' you know," cited Robin.

"We'll make you senior partner in the firm, Leila Greatheart," was Marjorie's generous proposal. "Harper, Page and Dean has a fine, dignified sound."

"Away with you!" Leila waved off the suggestion. "I am deaf to such a sound. Say no more, or I shall fly into one of my fierce frenzies. Now I am here not to rage, but to keep Midget in order, and conduct this meeting."

"*In order?*" Vera interrogated in an awful voice. "Kindly state *when* I have been out of order since this go-as-you-please session began."

"Not at all, Midget; not at all—as yet," Leila laid significant stress on "as yet." "So we may hope for the best and change the subject," she hastily added.

"It's high time it was changed," Vera said loftily.

Leila turned comical eyes upon the company. Then she continued: "Now we have the Irish play and the auction on the carpet. Soon we shall be giving Kathie's new play: 'The Knight of the Northern Sun.' Gentleman Gus will be featured in that. Kathie had finished the writing of it. Luciferous has already typed the parts. And I have picked a fine heroine. The Ice Queen is to play the part of Nageda, the Norse princess."

CHAPTER VI.

A TANTALIZING GLIMPSE

"Where did you collect the nerve to ask that ask?" Jerry admiringly demanded of Leila, following the shout of surprise from the others.

"I have nerve for any occasion," was the modest reply.

"I believe you. What did the Ice Queen say to you, or was she too icily iced for words? I get you that she must have made a 'yes' sign, in spite of her freezing frozenness."

"She said 'yes.' I went straight to the point with plenty of coolness in my own sweet Irish voice," Leila answered with a touch of grimness. "She loves to be a center of attraction. I have a good idea of her beauty and cleverness. She knows that. We made the bargain like two veterans. She does not wish for my friendship. I can live without hers. We have in Ireland our own proverb of fair exchange. It is: 'To exchange needs with your neighbor is nothing lost to him or you.'"

"In this instance it is everything gained," Marjorie blithely asserted. "You are the same old wonder, Leila Greatheart. I must make a list of these coming attractions now." She opened the small blue leather notebook which she was seldom without now wherever she happened to go on the campus. She wrote busily for a little, oblivious of the murmur of discussion going on around her.

"Three sure-fire attractions," she exulted, as she presently glanced up from her notebook.

"I've something to report, too. I've at last persuaded Miss Oliver to let us feature her in a musicale in Greek Hall. It's to come off a week from Friday evening." Robin's announcement was touched with pride.

It was the signal for another little burst of surprise. While Candace Oliver, the freshman musical genius who one of the Craig Hall girls had discovered, had on several occasions reluctantly played for Robin and a few other admiring students, she had steadily refused to appear on the college stage as a pianiste.

"Another obstacle surmounted. How did you do it? I thought I was too persuasive to be resisted, but she turned me down," commented Muriel.

"Oh, I asked her to let us feature her, every time I met her. I used all the nice pleasant arguments I could think of but without effect. The other day I happened to meet her at Baretti's. I introduced Signor Baretti to her. I was sitting at the same table with her and Baretti came up, as always, to speak to me. He only stayed a minute, but in that minute I remarked to him that Miss Oliver was a wonderful pianiste. He looked truly impressed and said in his odd way: 'I like hear you play som'time. When you play in Miss Page, Miss Dean's show, for help the dormitory. Miss Page, you come tell me when Miss Ol-ee-var play.' I smiled at Miss Oliver. She had turned red as a poppy. Then I said, sweet as cream: 'I surely *will* let you know, Signor Baretti.'"

"What did she say?" Ronny voiced the question that stood in six pairs of bright eyes.

"Oh, he trotted off just then, and I didn't give her time to say a word. I began telling her about him and how sincere his interest in the dormitory was, and how he had fought for Page and Dean, and how altogether great-spirited he was. She listened without saying much. She was half through luncheon when I sat down at her table. She left the restaurant as soon as she had finished her dessert. Next day I received a four line note from her. She said in it that she had changed her mind about not being featured at a musicale. 'I wish to do my part to help the dorm' girls,' was the line that made Robin execute a hornpipe."

"The infallible Guiseppe again to the rescue," Vera said lightly, yet with a certain pleased intonation which expressed the appreciation underlying it.

"Attraction number four." Amid the gratified murmur which followed Robin's recital, Marjorie set down the musicale in her book. "What is Miss Oliver's program, Robin? Of course you've seen her since you received her note." Marjorie knew that Robin was sure of her prize.

"Three Chopin numbers and Beethoven's 'Sonata Appassionata.' Phil is going to play one of Brahm's Hungarian dances and Jensen's 'Romance.' Verna Burkett is going to sing. She has a glorious contralto voice, and Reba Hoffman, that little blonde German dorm will give a 'cello number. I am anxious to exploit dorm talent, too. It's going to be a hummer of a program. I think we ought to charge two dollars apiece for the tickets, the same as we charge for our revues. What do you think about it, Marjorie?" Robin earnestly consulted her partner. "You know we only charged a dollar and a half for tickets for the last musicale."

"I don't believe two dollars a seat will be considered robbery. We always reserve free seats for the dormitory girls at all the shows. The other Hamiltonites can afford to pay two dollars apiece for the kind of entertainment we shall offer. They'd have to pay from two to three dollars apiece for good seats at a special benefit musicale wherever they might go," was Marjorie's candid reply. "I don't wish to seem priggish, but they could spend their allowance checks for no better cause."

"True as truth, good partner," Robin agreed, with a saucy little nod. "Oh, dear," she changed to plaintive in a twinkling. "I wish we might use the Hamilton Concert Hall for the musicale. Think of the money we'd take in. Greek Hall is hardly more than half as large."

"Why can't you use it?" asked Lucy Warner with crisp suddenness.

"No one has the nerve to ask Prexy for the use of it, my child." Vera bent a benign glance upon Lucy which contrasted oddly with her doll-like daintiness.

"Why not?" Lucy persisted.

"Prexy has yet to come to one of our shows, Luciferous," Marjorie said quietly. "We've always sent him tickets, and Mrs. Prexy and her friends have come to them. But he never has. He approves of the dormitory enterprise. He has been friendly with me on all occasions, but—" Marjorie smiled—"he never appears at our revues."

"It's the one thorn on Page and Dean's rosebush," laughed Robin. "Besides, Luciferous, we've never felt like trying to break into the regular college lecture and concert programs with our shows. It's more a matter of deference than anything else. If he had ever offered the hall to us, we'd have accepted the offer instanter. But he never has."

"I believe it never occurred to him," Lucy said bluntly. "I wish I'd known long ago. I'll ask him tomorrow for the use of it."

"Lu-ciferous!" Muriel beamed on Lucy with a radiance too joyous to be genuine. "You deserve a citation. That is you will deserve one if you put the Prexy problem across. Do so, and I will cite your good conduct tomorrow evening in this very room at precisely seven o'clock. You will receive a tin star, three whacks on the shoulder and a ticket to the Hamilton Movie Palace. Popcorn and pink lemonade will be served to all." Muriel effulgently included the rest of the party in the generous invitation.

The next five minutes were spent in jubilantly rushing Lucy. She received approving pats on the shoulders, pats on the back and pats on the head. Each Traveler tried to outdo the other in contributing funnily approving remarks. Muriel smilingly proposed raising Lucy to Jerry's and her shoulders and parading about the room with her. Jerry and Lucy both had strong objections to the honor walk.

"I wouldn't trust either of you to carry me two feet," Lucy declared mirthfully. "Now never mind rushing me further. Leila beguiled us here with the promise of hearing something extraordinary. I have yet to hear it."

"So I did." Leila surveyed the Travelers, whose attention had quickly returned to her, her bright blue eyes asparkle. "Now this is what I have to say."

As she laid her plan before her chums, a constant chorus of gurgles, giggles and chuckles accompanied her words. The instant she paused Jerry raised a not too loud cheer of approbation which the others echoed.

"I am indebted to you, Matchless Muriel, for suggesting the proper kind of refreshments. You may believe that popcorn and pink lemonade will be served at our party along with gum drops and peppermint sticks. I had not yet thought of the eats until you spoke. Now I shall get up a fine spread." Leila's tone conveyed her deep satisfaction.

"It will be oceans of fun." Muriel had already begun to laugh as she thought of what her part in the event should be.

"The gentlemen of the campus may have to hunt diligently for suitable wardrobe. I shall see about mine at once." Vera giggled softly.

Her naive remark was the signal for a fresh explosion of mirth. In a room further along the hall a girl moodily rested her pen to listen to the breath of laughter wafted faintly to her through walls and closed doors. Doris Monroe tried to frown at the distant sounds of harmonious comradeship. She found that she was not angry. She was despondent because she was lonely. She was beginning to glimpse a side of college life, wholly desirable, but, unfortunately for her, beyond her reach.

CHAPTER VII.

THE DARK TOWER

Doris Monroe had seen Marjorie and Jerry in the dining room of Wayland Hall that evening. She knew the Travelers were holding a social session in Leila's and Vera's room and somberly envied them their fun. Things had been distressingly dull for her since her return from the holiday vacation spent with Leslie Cairns in New York.

She had thoroughly enjoyed herself in New York after Mrs. Gaylord, Leslie's chaperon, had appeared at the Essenden, the apartment hotel in which Leslie had engaged the Dresden suite of rooms. Leslie, too, had been more agreeable during that short, blissful two weeks of fine dressing, expensive dinners, luncheons and theatres than Doris had known her to be either before or since the vacation.

The few times she had been in Leslie's company after their return to Hamilton, Leslie had been preoccupied, irritable and altogether unpleasant. She had been so patently uncongenial that Doris had preferred to keep away from her on the plea of study. This plea was at least sound. Doris had had her hands full for a time in trying to stave off being conditioned in mathematics.

She had known nothing of Leslie's downfall as a business woman. It was at least three weeks after Leslie had reluctantly obeyed her father's mandate and left Hamilton for New York before she had written Doris a letter from an apartment on Central Park West which Mrs. Gaylord had secured for the two as a residence.

In the letter Leslie had stated that she would return to Hamilton for a few days early in April. She had not, however, explained her sudden departure, nor had she mentioned the disruption of her garage enterprise. Doris had answered the letter, feeling secretly relieved that Leslie was not in Hamilton. She had a shrewd idea that Leslie's father might be responsible for Leslie's return to New York. She had heard enough of the conversation between Leslie and her chaperon on the occasion, when Mrs. Gaylord had arrived unexpectedly at the Essenden, to guess that Leslie and her father were not on very congenial terms.

Leslie had left Doris the Dazzler, the white car she was so fond of driving. She had said nothing in her letter about it, nor had she mentioned the sum of money which she had placed to Doris's account in a Hamilton bank. Doris had not yet been able to return the seventy-five dollars she had drawn of the five hundred Leslie had placed in bank to her credit. She was resolved on doing so before the close of college in June. Selfishly indifferent and indifferently selfish though she was she had a certain standard of honor. She had not ceased to regret having allowed Leslie to bank the five hundred dollars to her account.

Doris was not so anxious to return the Dazzler to Leslie. True she had no expectation of keeping it indefinitely. She hoped, however, that Leslie would allow her to use it until the close of college. She was able to pay for its up-keep from her allowance. Though she cared little for the freshies and sophs who made much of her, she frequently took one or more of them with her on her drives in the white car. Secretly she preferred her own company to theirs. She regarded them as more or less "silly" and continued to accept their adoration with bored sweetness.

Unwillingly she had discovered in herself a growing interest for the Travelers. Her keen perception could not fail to show her their undeniable claim to originality and cleverness. She admired, even liked Muriel, to whom she had, however, not spoken since before Christmas. Before their misunderstanding she had been on the verge of real fondness for Muriel. She now missed their former pleasant relation as roommates. At times she was tempted to lay aside her grievance and try to restore the old friendly footing.

Leila had approached Doris at the psychological moment. Doris was weary of being rushed by those for whom she entertained hardly more than casual interest. She had not the diversion of Leslie Cairns' companionship. She had persistently turned "dig" to the extent of putting herself beyond the immediate fear of a condition in mathematics. She was therefore ready to entertain with secret pleasure Leila's polite request for her appearance in "The Knight of the Northern Sun." She was actually eager to take the part of Nageda, the Norseland princess.

Outwardly she showed herself as coolly business-like as Leila during their brief interview. After she and Leila had separated she experienced a half sad regret because she appeared to be so thoroughly "out of it" with clever Miss Harper. She was sure Miss Harper cared nothing about her personally. She merely regarded her as a student; one best suited to play the part of Nageda.

"The Knight of the Northern Sun" was to be given on the evening of April thirtieth. It would be presented at least three weeks in advance of Leila's Irish play. The Candace Oliver musicale was to take place on the evening of April fourth. On the night of April eleventh Leila's "great idea" would furnish the entire college body of students with an evening's fun.

Such was the program the Travelers drew up. After the meeting came the usual spread, eaten in high spirits. Marjorie, Robin and Jerry stole downstairs several minutes after inexorable old ten-thirty had shrilled its loud emphatic nightly command for retiring. Very quietly the trio let themselves out the front door into the moonlight.

Marjorie and Jerry gallantly offered themselves as Robin's escorts across the moonlit campus to Silverton Hall. They took hold of her arms and paraded her between them, expatiating to her as they rushed her along at a hiking stride, on the value of their company. In front of Silverton Hall they lingered briefly for a last animated exchange of laughing pleasantries, then Jerry and Marjorie turned their steps toward the entrance at the east end of the campus which gave on the pike toward Hamilton Estates.

"It seems strange to be walking out of the campus gates at this time of night." Marjorie made this light observation as the two Travelers stepped from the college premises and out upon Hamilton Pike.

"We're enchanted, you know. We broke the spell for a little while this evening. There's the enchanted trail back to the good fairy's castle." Jerry pointed to the pike, shining and white under the moon's clear, burning lamp. "That's the way I've felt most of the time since we settled ourselves at the Arms."

"So have I. It's not only Hamilton Arms that seems enchanted. Hamilton Estates is like a fairy-tale kingdom," Marjorie added to Jerry's fancy.

"The Kingdom of Castles," Jerry instantly supplied. "And in the heart of the kingdom dwelt Goldendede, a fairy empress."

As they continued on their way to the Arms the pair amused themselves with the weaving of a fairy tale about Miss Susanna, Hamilton Estates and themselves as willing victims of enchantment.

"Bing! that nearly shattered the enchantment," grumbled Jerry as an automobile whisked past them from the direction in which they had come. "There's nothing fairy-like about a buzz-buggy. That particular one butted into our fairy tale and reu-ined it."

"Never mind. You've been truly inspired since we left the campus tonight, Jeremiah," Marjorie consoled. "Goldendede is a beautiful name for Miss Susanna. The Kingdom of Castles exactly suits Hamilton Estates. You couldn't have named this aloof collection of turreted gabled houses better."

"That's higher commendation than you ever gave the Bean Jingles. It makes up for your sad lack of appreciation of those gems. I am *so* mollified, Bean!" Jerry fairly purred gratification.

"I'd appreciate your art of jingling more, Jeremiah, if it were addressed to someone else. Leila or Ronny or Vera Jingles would be less personal."

"You have a grudge against your charming self, Bean," was Jerry's retort. "Forget it. Brooke Hamilton is to be celebrated in biography, why shouldn't Marjorie Dean be celebrated in verse. The first is not greater than the last in her own little way. The—"

"Say another word like that and I'll run off and leave you in the enchanted dark." Marjorie placed a light hand over Jerry's lips.

Jerry gently removed the restraining fingers and gave them a friendly squeeze. She kept Marjorie's hand in hers and the two walked on, arms swinging. "You're a resplendent goose," she said, "but you win. At least you do until the next time."

"Jerry, did you notice Miss Susanna's face today as she stood on the veranda waving to us?" Marjorie changed the subject with abruptness. "It was transfigured!"

"I noticed. I thought then that there could not be anything quite so wonderful as the return of happiness to a person who had been shut away from happiness as long as she had." Jerry turned suddenly serious. "And you began it, Marvelous Manager. You were the leaven—"

Marjorie dropped Jerry's hand and flashed away from her along the pike, a slim, flitting, shadowy figure. She was laughing softly to herself as she ran on for a few yards.

"I told you I'd run away from you." she reminded, as Jerry came speeding up to her. "I didn't propose to stay after hearing myself compared to a yeast cake."

The two had paused, breathless and laughing at one side of the pike. Their run had brought them just beyond the brightly lighted gate posts of Lenox Heath, a rambling, many gabled English manor house. Its powerful gate lights illuminated the pike for several hundred feet. Farther ahead of them it was dark and shadowy, in spite of the full moon's rays.

A few more steps would bring them to the part of the highway which skirted the Carden estate, forming its southern boundary. Formerly the pike at this point had extended between irregular embankments of stony earth which rose to a low height above the pike's smooth bed. It was at this particular part of the pike that Miss Susanna had narrowly escaped being run over by Lillian Walbert's car on a February afternoon of the previous year.

During the summer which followed the date of Miss Susanna's near accident, the right side of the pike which marked the northern boundary of the Clements estate had been leveled with the road bed by order of the Clements themselves. The low lumpy irregular ridge on the Carden side of the pike remained, flaunting itself in the face of improvement, a proof of Carden indifference and obstinacy. Because of it the Carden house and grounds appeared even more neglected and unkempt.

"It's good and dark here in spite of the moon." Jerry glanced up at the great arching limbs of the trees on the Carden side of the pike. A row of giant elms grew just inside the thick evergreen hedge which enclosed the Carden premises and gave the estate its name. Though still bare of leaves, the thick interlacing branches of the elms served as a screen against the moon's pale radiance.

"What a gloomy old dump the Carden estate is!" was Jerry's disapproving exclamation. "It looks like a ghost ranch."

"It's the Dark Tower in the Kingdom of Castles." This time Marjorie did the naming. "'Two Travelers to the Dark Tower came,'" she laughingly misquoted.

"Let's hope we don't see the horrors Childe Roland was supposed to have seen. Goodness knows *what* bogie horrified him. I should call 'Childe Roland' Browning's most aggravating poem. But this eerie spot is no place for a literary discussion. B-r-r-r! Let's beat it. I saw a white ghostly light flash out from behind that old house!"

Jerry did not accept her own proposal. Instead she stopped short, eyes trained on the pale flood of light. It emanated from a point behind the house and whitened a space to the left of the gloomy gray stone dwelling.

"Here comes your ghost, and in an automobile." Marjorie began to laugh. Two white eyes of light had appeared around the left hand corner of the house and were rapidly coming down the drive toward the watchers. "'Two goslings to the Dark Tower came—and saw a gasoline ghost,'" she mocked.

The watchers came abreast of the entrance gateway of the estate just as the car reached it. By its light they saw that the gates stood open. They hurried past them and drew close to the uneven ridge of earth in order to allow the automobile plenty of room to turn onto the pike. Instead of driving on, the solitary occupant stopped the machine at the edge of the pike just clear of the gateway.

The machine itself was a long, rakish-looking racing car. Its driver was a tall man, very broad of shoulder. He wore a long dark motor coat. A leather motor cap was pulled down over his forehead. Intent on his own affairs, he did not glance toward the two young women. He sprang from the racer and strode back to close the gates. He slammed them shut with an air which indicated proprietorship. Two or three long steps and he had returned to his car. He leaped into it, started it and was gone almost instantly around the curve of the pike which was the last outpost of the Carden estate. Just on the other side of it the estate of Hamilton Arms began.

"*Some ghost.* That's the first time I ever saw anyone emerge from that gloom patch, day or night. Now who do you suppose he was? If he's a visitor at Carden Hedge he must be visiting either himself or spooks. Maybe he's a Carden. Not that I care a hoot who he is, but one must have something to say about everyone." Jerry left the rough ground on which the two had been standing for the smoothness of the pike. "Come along, Bean. It will be midnight before we hit the castle," she predicted. "Ronny was right about this pair of Travelers."

"I wonder if he was one of the Cardens?" Marjorie's question contained a certain amount of curiosity. Since she had taken up the work of arranging the data for Brooke Hamilton's biography she had found enough allusions to the Carden family to give her a clear idea of what a thorn Alec Carden had been to Brooke Hamilton's flesh.

"He may be the son of Alec Carden. I mean the son who inherited Carden Hedge," she continued musingly. "This man in the racer wasn't young. I caught a fair view of his face in spite of the way he had his cap pulled down. Still he may be younger than I thought him at a glance, and the grandson of old Alec Carden."

"Why worry about it?" teased Jerry. She had caught the note of puzzled interest in Marjorie's voice.

"I'm not worrying. I'm wondering why that man's face looked so familiar. I'm sure I never saw him before."

"How can he look familiar to you if you've never before seen him?" inquired Jerry, with a chuckle.

"That's precisely what I'm wondering. Perhaps he resembles some one I know or have seen. I must ask Miss Susanna to describe John Carden, the son who lives at the Hedge. Here we are at our own castle. Next time we mustn't stay out so late, Jeremiah. I hope Miss Susanna hasn't stayed up to wait for us. She likes her early bedtime, you know."

Miss Susanna had elected to "stay up" to hear about Leila's "great" idea. They found her waiting for them in the library, wrapped in a trailing blue velvet dressing gown. She hustled them upstairs to don negligees and ordered them down to the library when they should have changed costume. There she brought them two little Chinese bowls of chicken consommé and a plate of salty crackers.

Both girls had eaten sparingly of the spread. After their moonlight walk they were really hungry, and the consommé was delicious. As they ate it and nibbled the crisp crackers they regaled Miss Susanna with a lively account of the evening's happenings. Interest in the Travelers' new plans for entertainments drove the incident of the unknown motorist completely from Marjorie's mind. Nor did she think of him again for some time afterward.

CHAPTER VIII.

A RETURN TO A FORBIDDEN LAND

"Leslie, is it really you? I'd been wondering why you hadn't answered my letter. I wrote you soon after I received your note." Doris Monroe's indifferent drawl was not in evidence as she answered the telephone. She was surprised and more pleased than she had thought she could possibly be to hear Leslie Cairns' voice on the wire. Leslie's arrival in Hamilton meant an immediate brightening of the bored existence Doris had been leading since her return from New York.

"I wrote you I'd surely be here in April," Leslie brusquely reminded, "and here I am."

"I'm *awfully* glad of it." Doris spoke with pleasing sincerity. "Is Mrs. Gaylord with you?"

"Ye-es." Leslie drawled the affirmation with exaggerated weariness. "How she does wish she wasn't. She nearly had a conniption when I told her we were going to make a flying trip to Hamilton. I'll meet you at the Colonial at four this P. M. You'll hear more of my history then. Bye." Leslie was gone.

Doris's beautiful face was a study as she turned from the telephone. She was a trifle amazed at her distinct pleasure in Leslie's unexpected arrival at Hamilton. Leslie had been so moodily unbearable after their return from the holiday vacation which they had spent in New York, Doris had felt relieved at the former's sudden disappearance from Hamilton and the subsequent receipt of Leslie's brief note from New York.

It was only recently that she had begun to miss Leslie and wish for her society. In spite of her ugly moods Leslie was possessed of an originality which Doris found singularly enlivening. No one could say more oddly funny things than Leslie when she chose to be humorous. Leslie never hesitated to pay extravagantly for whatever she happened to want. Doris admired in her what she considered Leslie's "adventurous spirit." She had been brought up to know her father's explorer friends. They were hardy, intrepid world wanderers of daring. She had listened to their tales of reckless adventuring into the unknown and gloried in the doings of these splendid captains of adventure. There were occasions when it appeared to her that Leslie showed something of the same adventurous, undaunted spirit.

As a matter of truth, Leslie was animated by this very spirit. She had directed it, however, into ignoble channels. What she chose to regard as strategy and daring were nothing other than trickery and lawlessness.

Doris knew little or nothing of Leslie's flagrant offenses as a student at Hamilton College. She had learned of the latter's expellment from college from Leslie herself. She had consequently never heard the rights of the affair. She had heard vague stories concerning it from Julia Peyton, Clara Carter and one or two juniors. The knowledge of Leslie's immense wealth had hampered even their gossip about the ex-student. The freshmen and the sophomores, who were Doris's chief companions, had entered Hamilton too late to be on the campus at the period before Leslie's and her chums' expulsion from college. They, therefore, knew not much about her.

The present junior and senior classes had been respectively the freshman and sophomore classes during Leslie's senior year at Hamilton, which had been also the year of her expulsion from college. At that particular time the attitude of the two lower classes had been one of horrified disapproval of the seventeen San Soucians who had been expelled from Hamliton for hazing a student. That was almost as much as any of them had ever learned about the affair. The girls who knew the disagreeable truth were Marjorie Dean and her intimates. Silence with them was honor. They knew a great many other derogatory facts about Leslie Cairns and her methods which they kept strictly sub rosa.

Doris was ready to welcome Leslie with warmth. She sorely lacked companions of interest. She had begun to grow bored to satiety by admiration. The freshies' and sophs' adoration for her was too superficial to be satisfying. They enjoyed rushing the college beauty. Each class liked to parade her on the campus and fête her at Baretti's, the Colonial or at their pet Hamilton tea shops as a triumphant class trophy. She was selfish, but not shallow; indifferent, but not vapid. It was in her composition to give as well as receive. Because she had been surfeited with adulation she had lately experienced a vague unrestful desire to turn from the knowledge of her own charms to an admiration of some one else.

First among the students of Hamilton she admired Leila Harper. Robin Page was her second "crush." Muriel made a third in a trio which had won her difficult fancy. None of these, however, were likely to become her friends. She would never make overtures to them. She was confident that they would never make further friendly advances to her.

Such a state of mind on her part augured a hearty welcome for Leslie. Doris hurried to her room after her last afternoon class, hastily got into the new fawn English walking suit, recently arrived from a Bond Street shop, and made a buoyant exit from the Hall and to the garage for the white car. It was a clear, sunshiny day. She thought Leslie might like to take a ride in the Dazzler. Leslie had probably hired a taxicab in which to come from town to the Colonial.

It was a very short distance from the garage to the Colonial. Arrived there, Doris saw a solitary car parked in front of the restaurant. It was a black roadster of newest type and most expensive make. She jumped to an instant conclusion that it must belong to Leslie.

Doris parked the Dazzler behind the roadster and went into the tea room to meet Leslie. She found her seated at one of the several square mission oak tables engaged in a languid perusal of a menu card.

"How are you, Goldie? Have a seat at the table and a bite with yours truly." Leslie waved Doris into the chair opposite her. Then she stretched an arm lazily across the table and offered Doris her hand.

"Very well, thank you, Leslie. How have you been getting along?" Doris returned, with only a shade of her usual drawl. "I *am* glad to see you. I have missed you."

"A good miss." Leslie shrugged an accompaniment to her laconic comment. "Were you surprised to hear me on the 'phone?"

"Of course. I was surprised when you wrote me from New York. I had no idea you had left Hamilton. I was afraid of being conditioned in math. I was studying like mad and hadn't time just then to call you on the telephone at the hotel. I knew you were very busy." So far as she went Doris was truthful.

"Oh, forget it. I believe what you say, Goldie, but you might have added that you were all fed up with me. I know I had a beastly grouch after the New York trip. It had teeth and claws. I had business trouble. That sneaking carpenter who is trying to swing the dormitory job for Bean and her precious Beanstalks coaxed all my men over to the Beggar Ranch. He told them a lot of fairy stories, I suppose. Anyway, I had to send for one of my father's best men, an Italian financier, who understands Italian peasants. Even he couldn't undo the mischief that scamp, Graham, had done.

"I finally had to send for my father. He fired the whole shooting match. I'm done with that garage flivver. My father said it wouldn't pay me very well in the end. He was sore at me for wasting my time around this burg. He tried to make me promise I'd go to New York and never think about Hamilton again. He can't stand the college since the precious Board gave me such an unfair deal."

"Why, that's dreadful, Leslie; about your garage I mean." Doris had a certain amount of sympathy for Leslie. She was not specially interested in business, but she decided that Leslie had been badly treated.

"I'll say it is," Leslie made grim response. "Oh, never mind. I'm still worth a few dollars. Did you see my new car out in front?"

"Yes—I had an idea that car must belong to you. It suggested you to me at first sight." Doris smiled across the table at her returned friend. "I had no idea you'd have a car. I brought the Dazzler on purpose. I thought we might like to take a ride."

"Gaylord and I came here from New York in that car," Leslie informed with an inflection of pride. "My father doesn't know I'm here. He sailed for Europe last Thursday. I know positively that he went, too. I was at the dock and saw his steamer cut loose from Manhattan."

"Were you?" Doris exhibited her usual polite reticence regarding Leslie's father. Long since she had discovered that Leslie did not like to answer questions about him. "It is rather a long drive from New York, isn't it. Your motor coat and hat are chic."

"So is your suit. I suppose it floated straight across the pond to you. My coat came from the Clayham, in New York. But it's some bang-up English shop, now let me tell you." Leslie showed brightening satisfaction of her own greenish-gray motor coat and round hat of the same material.

Leslie's own remarks about her father were "fairy stories" so far as her having seen him entered into them. She had not seen him, nor had she received any letters from him other than the peremptory one in which he had scathingly reprimanded her and ordered her to New York. Nevertheless she *had* seen him sail for Europe in the "*Arcadia*," though he had not known of her presence on the dock when the steamer cleared.

She had gone to the dock in a cheap tan rain-coat, a red worsted Tam o'Shanter cap and a pair of shell-rimmed glasses. Mingling with the crowd on the dock she was confident her disguise was effective. Her father's manager, Mr. Carrington, had furnished her with the information of the date and hour of her father's departure for Europe. She had not seen him since the day when she had called at her father's offices. Neither had he seen her father for more than a few minutes at a time during which no mention of Leslie had been made. He had been led by her to believe that she had planned a pleasant steamer surprise for her father. He had therefore kept his own counsel and his promise to Leslie. He had sent her a note to the Essenden which had been duly forwarded to her new address.

"I should think you'd rather be in New York than here." Doris gave a half envious sigh. "There's nothing here of interest off the campus."

"Oh, I had to come here while Peter the Great was away." Leslie volunteered this much of an explanation of her visit. "I must get a line on what was done on the garage so I'll know just how much money I put into it. My father will want to know that right off the bat if he offers it for sale as it stands. You and I will have some bully rides and drives while I'm here, Goldie. I shan't be such a grouch as I was right after Christmas. How are things at the knowledge shop? How is Bean? Had any fusses with her or her Beanstalks lately?" Leslie's expression grew lowering as she mentioned Marjorie.

"Miss Dean and Miss Macy aren't at Wayland Hall now. They're staying at Hamilton Arms. I don't know whether they are coming back to the Hall again or not." Doris had expected the information might elicit surprise from her companion. She smiled in faint amusement of Leslie's astonished features, then added the crowning bit of news. "Miss Dean was chosen by Miss Hamilton to write Brooke Hamilton's biography."

CHAPTER IX.

A WILD PLAN

"What-t? Do you know what you're saying?" Leslie's tones rose higher.

"I ought to know. I've heard nothing else since she left the Hall for Hamilton Arms." Doris's tone was the acme of weariness. "It wouldn't have been surprising to hear that President Matthews had been asked to write Brooke Hamilton's biography," she continued. "The idea of *Miss Dean* as his biographer is, well—*ridiculous*."

"It's pure bosh," Leslie said contemptuously. "She's a tricky little hypocrite. She's managed to curry favor with that wizened old frump at Hamilton Arms. The last of the Hamiltons! She looks it. I heard when I was at Hamilton that she was sore at the college; that she had all the dope for Brooke Hamilton's biography but wouldn't come across with it. I presume Bean slathered her with deceitful sweetness until she grew dizzy with her own importance and renigged."

"I don't like Miss Dean." Doris's fair face clouded. "I'm glad she's not at the Hall any longer. Miss Harper and her other friends don't appear to miss her much, or Miss Macy either. They have parties in one another's rooms almost every night."

"They have found they can live without her," was Leslie's satiric opinion. "You certainly have handed me news, Goldie."

"Oh, that's only a beginning," Doris declared, well pleased with Leslie's appreciation. "The other night Miss Dean and Miss Macy were at the Hall to dinner. Afterward they were in Miss Harper's room with their crowd. They had a high old time talking and laughing. I could hear them, but not very plainly. They were planning shows, though. Since then a notice for a piano recital, featuring Candace Oliver, a freshie musical genius, has appeared on all the bulletin boards. Since that notice there has come another of an Irish play by Miss Harper. It's to be given in May. The name of the play and the cast hasn't yet been announced. Miss Harper is awfully tantalizing. She always waits until campus curiosity is at fever height about her plays before she gives out any more information."

"She's a foxy proposition." Leslie showed signs of growing sulkiness. Her earlier affability had begun to wane at first mention of Marjorie Dean. Next to Marjorie, Leila Harper was registered in her black books.

"She's clever, Leslie; not foxy," Doris calmly corrected. She went on to tell Leslie of the part Leila had asked her to play in "The Knight of the Northern Sun."

Leslie's deep-rooted jealousy of the two girls who were college successes where she had been a rank failure rushed to the surface. "Leila Harper has nerve to ask you to be in a play when she knows you are a friend of mine. I see her game. She knows just how useful you can be to her in her confounded old play. It's some feather in her theatre bonnet to keep the college beauty at her beck and call. She has planned to break up our friendship by flattering you into believing you are a dramatic wonder. Bean is probably back of Harper's scheme. She can't and never could bear to see me enjoy myself."

Leslie jerked out the final sentence of her tirade against Leila with angry force. Her face had darkened in the jealous way which invariably reminded Doris of the driving of thunder clouds across a graying sky.

"Miss Harper was impersonal in asking me to be in the play," Doris defended. The sea shell pink in her cheeks had deepened perceptibly. "She dislikes me. I know she wants me in the cast because she thinks I'd be a feature. You see I'm the true Norse type. The heroine of the play is a Norse princess. I want to be in the play because I like to be in things. I'll enjoy the praise and the excitement. I may go on the English stage when I have been graduated from Hamilton. My father would not object if I were to play in a high class London company."

"The same old Goldie who cares for nobody but herself." Leslie gave vent to a sarcastic little snicker. "Why not take up with Bean, too?"

"Oh, Leslie, don't be hateful," Doris said with an air of resigned patience. "You know I detest Miss Dean. Nothing could induce me to take up with her. It's different with Miss Harper. She's not American, you know. She is so cosmopolitan in manner. She is really more my own style. But, of course, she's hopelessly devoted to that Sanford crowd of girls."

"Don't mention Sanford to me. I hate the name of that collection of one-story huts," Leslie exploded fiercely. "You ought to detest Bean, considering the way she has treated me. If she had been half as square as she pretends to be she would have put the kibosh on old Graham, just like that, when he began hiring my men away from my architects. My father said the whole business was a disgrace. He said there was no use in my trying to buck against an institution. That's what Bean's pull amounts to. She has both Prexy and that ancient Hamilton relict to back her."

"If Miss Dean knew that her architect was hiring your men away from your architects, and ignored the fact for her own business interests then she must be thoroughly dishonorable," Doris said flatly.

"If—if—There you go," sputtered Leslie, wagging her head, her shaggy eyebrows drawn together. "No 'if' about it. She knew. You talk as though you wanted to believe her honorable. Well, she isn't, never was; never will be. It makes me furious to think that she should go nipping around the campus as a college arc light while I wasn't even allowed a look at a sheepskin. Too bad I couldn't have learned some of her pretty little dodges. I'd have been able to slide out of the hazing racket. I'll tell you something you don't know. Bean could have helped us when the Board sent for her by refusing to go to Hamilton Hall to the inquiry. Not Bean. She went, and made such a fuss about pretending she didn't care to talk that it made us appear ten times as much to blame as we really were."

"If—" Doris hastily checked herself. "She seems to have tried her best to down you, Leslie. But, why?" Her green eyes directed themselves upon Leslie with a disconcerting steadiness.

Leslie gave a short laugh. "I used to ask myself that," she replied with a sarcastic straightening of her lips. "Now I understand her better. She was jealous and wanted to be the whole show, all the time. She is deep as a well. Take my word for it. I know her better than I wish I knew her." She shook her head with slow effective regret.

"I'll surely remember what you've said about her." Doris meant what she said. She had been distinctly shocked at both instances which Leslie had cited of Marjorie Dean's treachery. What she desired most now was that Leslie should drop the discussion of her grievances.

This Leslie was not ready to do. She continued on the depressing topic for several more minutes. Then she began asking Doris questions concerning the subject of Brooke Hamilton's biography. Doris knew only what she had already imparted to Leslie concerning it.

"None of the students know the details concerning it except Miss—I mean, the Travelers," she finally said desperately. She stopped short of mentioning Marjorie's name again. She did not care to start Leslie anew. "I imagine there really isn't much else to know besides what I've already told you."

"Don't you ever believe it," was the skeptical retort. "But I don't blame you, Goldie, for what you don't know."

"Thank you." Doris shrugged satiric gratitude. Glad to turn the conversation into a lighter strain she continued gaily: "We're soon going to have a general lark on the campus. The whole college crowd is to be in it. It's to be a 'Rustic Romp.' One-half of the girls are to dress up as country maids; the other half as country swains. In order to be sure of an even number of couples each student has to register her choice as maid or swain. If not enough girls register as swains then some of the maids will have to change their minds and do duty as gallants. Miss Evans, a rather nice senior, has charge of the registration. And it's to be a masquerade!" Doris's exclamation contained pleased anticipation.

"Wonderful." Leslie chose to be derisive. Underneath envious interest prompted her to ask; "Whose fond, fertile flight of foolishness was that? Mickie Harper's or Pudge and Beans?"

"I don't know whose inspiration it was. Probably the seniors had the most to do with it." Doris again steered the talk toward peaceful channels.

"Hm-m." Leslie glanced at Doris, then at the luncheon which the waitress was now placing before them on the table. She gazed abstractedly at the appetizing repast. Her eyes traveled slowly back to Doris. Suddenly she broke into one of her fits of silent, hob-goblin merriment. "I think I'll attend that hayseed carnival myself," she announced in a tone of defiant boldness.

CHAPTER X.

CLAIMING A PROMISE

"What do you mean?" Slightly mystified for an instant it then broke upon Doris that Leslie was in earnest. She was actually entertaining a wild idea of attending the coming romp behind the shelter of a mask. "You couldn't do that—er—it would be—unwise," she stammered. Dismay flashed into her green eyes.

"Why couldn't I?" The question vibrated with obstinacy. "Who except you would know me?"

"U-m-m; no one would know you while you were masked, I suppose. When it came time to unmask—"

"I'd not be in the gym at unmasking time," Leslie interrupted decisively. "I'd be out of that barn and away before the signal came to unmask."

Doris eyed Leslie doubtfully. Her first shock of dismay at the announcement had subsided. She was still swayed by caution as she said slowly: "It would be awfully risky for you. At the Valentine masquerade no one knew when the call to unmask was coming. That's the way it will be at the romp."

"At the Valentine masquerade when *I* was at Hamilton the time for unmasking was nine-thirty." The corners of Leslie's wide mouth took on an ugly droop.

"I know that is the way it used to be," Doris hastily re-assured. "At the last masquerade the freshies asked the junior committee to make the unmasking time a surprise. It proved to be a lot of fun. It will be done again this time. I'm almost sure it will."

"What if it should be? Don't imagine that I can't watch my step. I'd not be caught."

"Suppose you were dancing when the call to unmask came? You'd have to leave your partner instantly and run like a deer for the door. Suppose you were caught on the way to the door and unmasked by a crowd of girls? The freshies are terrors at that sort of thing. They are always out for tom-boy fun. You'd not care to have such an embarrassing thing happen to you." Doris chose to present to Leslie a plain supposition of what might happen to her as an uninvited masker at the romp.

"Leave it to me to make a clever get-away," was Leslie's boast. "I'd be safe for five or six dances. That would be as long as I'd care to stay in the gym. It's wearing a hayrick costume that strikes me as having some pep to it. The adventure of breaking into the knowledge shop and enjoying myself under the noses of Prigville, without any of the inhabitants knowing who I am, appeals to me."

Unwittingly she had appealed to the side of Doris most in sympathy with her bold plan. Doris had been born and bred to understanding and approval of adventure. "I understand the way you feel about it, Leslie," she began. "If I were certain that—"

"Oh, forget that I mentioned dressing up to you!" Leslie exclaimed with savage impatience. "You've said more than once that you'd be pleased to do anything you could for me, *at any time*. I thought you would help me a little to play this joke on Prigville. Never mind. I'll ask only one thing of you. If you *should* happen to recognize me on the night of the haytime hobble, kindly don't publish it among the prigs."

"Leslie." Doris put dignified reproach into the response. "You know I would never betray you. I'm perfectly willing to help you carry out your plan, provided there's no danger to either of us in it."

"Danger of what?" came the sarcastic question. "No danger to you. Let me do a little supposing. Suppose we went together to the gym; you as a maid, and I as your swain. Suppose I failed to make a get-away and was unmasked by a bunch of smart Alecs. I'd probably not be near you when the signal came to unmask. I'd not bother you after the grand march. There'd be so many hey Rubes in the gym no one would remember our coming in together. That lets you out, doesn't it? You should falter. Have a heart, Goldie!" Leslie had grown satirically persuasive.

Doris sat studying the situation in silence. She had colored afresh at Leslie's pointed inference that she was more concerned for her own security from possible mishap at the romp than for that of Leslie herself. She hated the sarcastic reminder flung at her by Leslie that she had promised a favor on demand and was now not willing to keep her word. As Leslie had presented the situation to her there could be no risk to her. Leslie was more than able to look out for her own interests. To help Leslie now meant not only the keeping of her promise. It was a singularly easy way of keeping it.

"I'd rather you'd turn me down now than next year," Leslie sneered as Doris continued silent.

"I'll help you, Leslie." Doris spoke stiffly, ignoring her disgruntled companion's sneer.

"Come again." Leslie cupped an ear with her hand, mockery in the gesture, but triumph in her small dark eyes.

"I said I would help you." Doris repeated her first statement in an even stiffer tone. She would not permit Leslie to break down her poise.

"Good for you. You won't be sorry. Help me to put over this stunt on Prigville and I'll give you the Dazzler for your own." Leslie was buoyantly generous in her delight at having gained her own way.

"I don't want any such reward. That's just the trouble with you, Leslie. You are always offering me so much more than I can ever return. I wish you were going to the dance, to stay all evening and have a good time with the others." Doris sincerely meant the wish.

"You know whose fault it is that I can't." Leslie shrugged significantly. "Now I must plan my costume." She straightened in her chair with a faint sigh. "I'll sport blue overalls, a brown and red gingham shirt, large plaid, with no collar; a turkey-red cotton hankie, a big floppy hayseed hat and a striped umbrella." She chuckled as she enumerated these items of costume.

"I had thought seriously of going as a swain, but decided against it. I'd rather look pretty. I have a certain reputation to keep up on the campus. I'd prefer not to caricature myself."

"You make me smile, Goldie. How you worship that precious beauty reputation of yours! You may be right about it. I presume you are."

Leslie's rugged face grew momentarily downcast. She was thinking morosely that if, like Doris, she had been half as careful in whom she trusted and to what risks she lent herself when at Hamilton she might have escaped disgrace.

"I know I am." Doris was emphatical. She noted the gloomy change in Leslie's features and understood partly what had occasioned it. Those four words, "I presume you are," made more impression on Doris than any other reference to her college trouble or against Marjorie Dean, which she had ever before heard Leslie make. It held a compelling, resigned inference of unfair treatment at the hands of others. Those others were of course Miss Dean and her friends. Doris allowed herself to jump to that conclusion. She had fostered jealous disdain of Marjorie until it had become antipathy. She knew Leslie's faults, but she chose to overlook them. She had sometimes regarded Leslie's accusations against "Bean" as overdrawn. Now she felt more in sympathy with Leslie's standing grudge against Marjorie Dean than at any time since she had known Leslie.

CHAPTER XI.

A RUSTIC DISASTER

The evening of April eleventh saw Hamilton campus in the possession of a social throng, large, rural and hilarious. The spring twilight was scarcely ready to drop faint lavender shades over departed day when from the various student houses on the big green issued veritable country bumpkins in festival attire. They appeared singly, in twos, threes, quartettes and straggling groups.

Fortunately for the rovingly-inclined bands of rural pleasure-seekers the night was warm and balmy. In the mild fragrant spring air, the giggling maids flaunted their bright calicos and ginghams, unhidden in their cotton glory by shawl, coat or cape.

The gallant swains who dotingly accompanied the flower-hatted or sun-bonneted, aproned ladies were a sturdy, rugged-looking lot in their blue or brown overalls, flannel or gingham shirts, brilliant cotton neck handkerchiefs and wide-brimmed straw field hats or weather-stained sombreros. A few ambitious rustic youths had appeared in their own fond weird conception of party attire. They were amazing and wonderful to behold.

"These happy hecks at Hamilton certainly have small feet," remarked a stocky rustic in a faded pink gingham shirt, a blue and white checked overall, broad, square-toed low shoes, a bright green neckerchief and a narrow-rimmed, round straw hat with a hole in the crown through which a lock of brown hair appeared, standing straight up. The accompanying mask was a round false face with very red cheeks and high arching brows.

"Well, they can't help it. If they hide 'em with brogans how can they dance with the lady hecks?" demanded a tall bumpkin in what he was now proudly exhibiting on the campus as "my horse clothes."

"Te, he he," giggled the stocky rustic. "Truly, Muriel Harding, I never saw you look so funny before in all my life."

"Sh-h-h, Jeremiah. I don't know how you knew me. Since you do, keep it dark. Some horse clothes! Have one of my cards." Muriel handed Jerry a correspondence card in a violent shade of pink. In the center of it was written: "Horsefield Hanks, Jockey and Post Master, Jayville."

Jerry continued to giggle at Horsefield Hanks' gala adornment. It consisted of a bright blue flannel shirt, a broad red leather belt, baggy brown trousers tucked into a pair of boot-modeled goloshes, a rusty black cutaway coat and a red and white striped jockey cap with a wide front peak. The mask was a false face of particularly ferocious expression. To look at Horsefield Hanks was not only to laugh. It was a signal to keep on laughing.

"Where is Marjorie?" Muriel inquired as she turned from bending a killing glance upon two hurrying maids, evidently intent on joining their swains. The two called a mirthful: "Hello, sweetness. Where did your face grow?" and whisked on their way.

"Gone over to the Hall to meet Robin. She has on a fine check yellow and white gingham dress trimmed with little yellow ruffles, white stockings and slippers and a white ruffled organdie hat with long yellow ribbon strings."

"I'll certainly know her if I see her. Vera is too cute for words. She has two overalls on, one over the other, to make her look fat. They're blue and her blouse is white. She has a black alpaca coat on, too. She managed to get hold of a funny little pair of copper-toed boots. She has built them up inside until she is at least three inches taller. She won't be easily recognized." Muriel rattled off the description in a low laughing voice. "Ronny has on a pale blue calico. It comes down to her heels. She has black slippers and stockings, a ruffled blue sunbonnet and a white kerchief folded across her shoulders. Lucy's dressed in the same style except her dress is lavender. Leila is a maid, but I haven't been able to pick her out yet. Now how in the world did you know that I was I?" Muriel demanded.

"I knew the most ridiculous costume I saw would be yours," chuckled Jerry. "You're so funny, you're positively idiotic."

"Then I'm likely to win the prize for having the funniest costume. Won't that be nice? Come on, Hayfoot, that's what you look like. Let's go out in the world and hunt up Strawfoot. I presume we'll be mobbed before we've gone far for not having our rustic maids along with us. Anyhow let's brave the jays and jayesses as long as we can." Muriel politely offered Jerry an arm. "I'm to meet Candace Oliver at seven-thirty at the Bean holder. I'm a gentleman jockey of leisure until then. The post office was closed early today. Jayville will have to wait for its mail."

The gallant pair had not proceeded fifty feet from their reconnoitering place before they were surrounded by a crowd of swains and maids and rushed over the green as prisoners to be apportioned to the first two swainless maids the company chanced to encounter.

Meanwhile a rustic gentleman in wearing apparel becoming to one of his lowly station had just made a very stealthy entrance to the campus from the extreme eastern gates. He had cautiously stepped from a smart black roadster which was parked a little way from the gates, but well off the highway. Before he had ventured to step from the car he had left the steering seat and disappeared into the tonneau of the machine, then simply a motorist in a voluminous leather motor coat, goggles and a leather cap.

From the back of the car had presently emerged a typical jay in blue overalls, and a loud-plaided, collarless, gingham shirt of green, blue and red mixture. He wore a turkey-red handkerchief, knotted about the neck, an immense flopping hat of yellowish straw, white socks and carpet slippers with worsted embroidered fronts. In one hand he clutched firmly a huge red and yellow striped umbrella. The mask, which Leslie had ordered sent to her from New York, was a very pink and white face, utterly insipid, with three flat golden curls pasted on the low forehead. Its expression, one of cheerful idiocy, was as distinctly as mirth-inspiring as was the fierce face of Horsefield Hanks. In fact it would have been hard to decide which of the two get-ups was the funnier.

One swift glance about her to assure herself of a clear coast and Leslie made a dash for the campus gates. She was through the gateway in a twinkling. She did not stop until she had put a little distance between herself and the gates. Then she paused, turned, critically surveyed the highway, the portion of the campus immediate to her and lastly her car. She was hardly content to leave it there, but there was no other way. It was well out of the path of other machines, either coming or going on the pike. She could but hope that no one would make off with it. She reflected with a wry smile that there were still a few more cars to be bought, though she might happen to lose that one. As usual she was prepared to pay lavishly for her fun.

She hurried straight on across the campus past Silverton Hall and in the direction of Acasia House. It was the most remote from the gymnasium of all the campus houses. She and Doris had agreed to meet there, making the appointment late enough to miss Acasia House rustics when they should set out for the gymnasium. Doris had telephoned her that afternoon and made the final arrangement for their rendezvous. They were to meet behind a huge clump of lilac bushes just budding into leaf.

As she came abreast of the lilac bushes a dainty figure in white dimity, imprinted with bunches of violets stepped forth to meet her. Doris's charming frock had a wide dimity sash and her dimity hat, trimmed with bunches of silk violets, had long violet ribbon strings. She wore flat-heeled black kid slippers and white silk stockings of which only a glimpse showed beneath her long gown.

One look at Leslie's inane false face and she burst into laughter. "Such a face!" she gasped mirthfully. "The funniest one I've seen since I left the Hall tonight."

Leslie lifted the spreading hat and disclosed to Doris a yellow wig which matched the curls pasted to her mask. "My face is my fortune," she announced humorously.

"It's too funny for words. I'm almost afraid we may be rushed." Doris cast an anxious glance at the not far distant crowd.

"Am I so funny as all that?" Leslie asked in gratification.

"You are quite extraordinarily funny," Doris assured. "The crowd on the campus has been going it strong ever since dinner. They're awfully frisky. Once they get into the gym they'll be wanting to dance. Then we won't be in danger. There's to be a prize given for the funniest costume. Too bad you can't stay in the gym long enough to win it."

"Oh, I don't want it. I only want a little fun," Leslie said.

Warily the pair skirted the crowd and went on to the gymnasium. Leslie's funny face immediately challenged the attention of a number of frisky couples parading the great room. They began flocking about herself and Doris, asking foolish questions in a gleeful effort to learn her identity. She remained mute for which Doris was thankful. Her vacant smiling mask merely continued to beam upon her hilarious questioners.

The Hamtown Gilt Medal Band and Orkestry were already in their corner, importantly ensconced behind a white pasteboard picket fence. They alone of the ruralites were unmasked. They were simple geniuses of music in overalls, gay-checked shirts and high-crowned haying hats of rough straw, speckled green and red. Strings of richly gilded pasteboard medals struggled across each musician's manly chest; they testified eloquently of past musical achievement. A large gilt-lettered sign, high on a standard flaunted the proud legend: "We have won all the medals in Hamtown for the past forty years. The only other band was a hand organ. Notice our decorations."

The leader and first violin of this renowned group of musicians was tall and rather blonde, with an imposing blonde goatee and an artistic sweep of curled blonde mustache. His companion players were hardly less well supplied with whiskers, mustaches and even side burns. In direct apposition to the rustic youths of the community of Hamtown they presented a decidedly mature, dignified appearance. They seemed complacently well aware of their musical superiority over their humbler companions and gave themselves plenty of airs.

At intervals about the spacious gym were little open booths where popcorn fritters, salted peanuts, stick candy, apples and oranges, molasses taffy and pink lemonade were sold. In each booth a masked rustic maid presided, keeping a lynx eye on her wares.

After the orchestra had tuned up with considerable scraping, sawing and tooting they burst into the rallying strains of the grand march. Doris heard the sound of the music with patent relief. She had grown more and more uneasy for fear that Leslie might forget her role of silence and blurt out a remark in her characteristic fashion. Anyone who had known her in the past would be likely to recognize her voice.

Doris had suggested that it would be better for they two to dance together the few numbers before the unmasking for which Leslie dared remain. To this Leslie would not hear. She craved freedom to roam about the gymnasium by herself and dance with whom she fancied. She and Doris walked through the grand march together and danced the first number. Then Leslie left Doris, who was being singled out by two or three husky farmer boys for attention, and strolled down the gymnasium, her striped umbrella under one arm.

Behind the fatuously-smiling blonde face her small dark eyes were keeping a bright watch on the revelers. She wondered where Bean and her Beanstalks were and tried to pick them out by height and figure. She decided that a maid in a pale pink lawn frock was Marjorie and promptly kept away from her. When the music for the second dance began she made her bow to a slim sprite in fluffy white who accepted with a genuine freshie giggle.

Encouraged by her success as a beau Leslie danced the next and still the next, each time with a different partner. She was a good dancer, and led with a sureness and ease quite masculine. After a couple of turns about the room Leslie had been obliged to discard her umbrella. She had boldly set it up inside the orchestra's picket fence where it would be less likely to attract the attention of prankish wags.

At the beginning of the fifth dance Leslie was not yet ready to go. She glanced at the wall clock which stood at five minutes to nine. It was still too early for unmasking. She believed herself safe for at least two more dances after the one about to begin. She started toward a group of two or three disengaged maids.

Suddenly from the farther end of the gymnasium a cry arose which Leslie mistook for "Unmask." It threw her into a panic. She forgot in her dismay that Doris had said the signal for unmasking would be the blast of a whistle. What she remembered instead was her striped umbrella. She was only a few steps from the orchestra corner. She made a frantic rush to it, reached over the low picket fence and snatched up the umbrella. She turned away, not noticing that she had laid low a section of the fence. She hurried across the floor, bent only on reaching the door.

"Oh!" A forceful exclamation went up as she crashed against a couple who had begun to dance. The force of the collision fairly took the breath of all three girls. Leslie made an unintentional backward step. The umbrella slid from under her arm toward the floor just as the jostled swain and his lady were about to move on. It tripped the rustic gallant neatly and he sprawled forward full length on the highly waxed floor, dragging his partner with him.

CHAPTER XII.

A RANK OUTSIDER

"What a clumsy creature you are!" The fallen gallant scrambled up from the floor and delivered the opinion in a feminine voice. It was shrill and wrathful. It rose in its shrillness above the rhythmic melody of the orchestra. "It's both inconsiderate and dangerous in you to carry such a large umbrella onto the floor. Your face and your behavior go nicely together."

"Beg your pardon for upsetting you, but keep your opinion to yourself." Leslie began the reply with forced politeness, but ended her words almost in a hiss. Behind her simpering mask she was a dark fury. "I never allow anyone to speak in that tone to me."

"How do you propose to prevent my saying what I please?" came back tauntingly from the belligerent swain. His partner, a slender, graceful figure in a pale yellow gingham gown placed a gently arresting hand on her angry gallant's arm. It was shaken off with instant hateful impatience.

"I don't propose to do that. Nothing short of a clamp could keep you from shrieking." Leslie had changed in a twinkling to rude insolence. "I'll have mercy on my ear drums and beat it."

"Wha-a-t?" The angry swain's voice had suddenly changed key. It had lowered in a mixture of amazed, disapproving conviction.

The utterance of that one amazed word acted upon Leslie like a sudden dash of cold water. She wheeled and swaggered on down the room with an air of elaborate unconcern. It was entirely make-believe. Her heart was thumping with dismay. She had spoken after having vowed within herself that whatever might happen at the romp she would remain mute. More, she was afraid she had been recognized by the student whom she had unwittingly tripped up with her umbrella. Something in those higher pitched tones had sounded familiar. She could not then remember, however, of whom they reminded her.

She had turned away from the quarrel just in time. Attracted by the commotion at that part of the gymnasium more than one pair of dancers had steered toward the accident center. Some of these now headed Leslie off in her perturbed journey down the room. They collected about her with mischievous intent, hemming her in and calling out to her.

"Such a pretty boy!" "Hello, April smiles!" "Wait a minute, puddeny-woodeny!" "I'm crazy about you!" were some of the pleasantries hurled at her. Under other circumstances Leslie would have laughed at the extravagances. Now she was growing worried for her own security from identification. She was now in precisely the situation against which Doris had warned her. Suppose the call to unmask were to come just then? She resolved desperately that, unheeding it, she would bolt for the door.

Meanwhile the tripped-up rustic was sputtering to his dainty partner in a manner which indicated trouble to come for Leslie.

"I wouldn't stand such insolence from another student, much less from an intruder," Julia Peyton was saying wrathfully. "I wouldn't—"

"Try to forget the matter, Miss Peyton," urged a soft voice.

"I shan't. Who are you, and how do you happen to know me?" demanded Julia rudely. "*You* don't know who that mask is. I *do*. She has no invitation or right to be here tonight. It's against all Hamilton tradition. Doris Monroe is to blame for this outrage. She has helped that horrid Miss Ca—"

"I am Miss Dean, Miss Peyton," came the interruption, low, but vibrating with sternness. "You will please not mention the name you were going to say."

"I'll do as I please about that. I'll do more. I'll expose that Miss Cairns before she has a chance to leave here. I know who's to blow the whistle for unmasking. She is a sophie friend of mine. I'll ask her to blow it now. Then we'll see what Miss Cairns will do."

Before Marjorie could stop her she had started up the room on a hunt for the sophomore who had been detailed to blow the unmasking whistle. A dismayed glance after Julia, then Marjorie followed her. There was but one thing she could do. She must follow Julia and discover to which sophomore had been intrusted the signal detail. Each class had been given a certain amount of the details for the romp. Among sophomore details was the sounding of the unmasking signal.

Unaware that she was being followed by Marjorie, Julia had gone on a tour of the room, searching this way and that, with spiteful eagerness. She now had a stronger motive for exposing Leslie than the latter's offense against tradition. She was determined to be even with Doris for having "almost" snubbed her on numerous occasions. It would not reflect to Doris's credit to be named as the student who had smuggled into the gym a girl who had been expelled from Hamilton.

The sophomore who was to blow the whistle was Jane Everest. Dressed in a befrilled frock of apricot dotted swiss, Jane formed a bright spot of color among the pale blues and pinks which was easily picked out. Julia had little trouble locating her. Marjorie, now not more than three yards behind Julia, reached the pair almost as soon as Julia hailed Jane. The two had met before that evening. Each knew the other's costume.

"Who do you think is here tonight?" Julia caught Jane's arm. This time she took the precaution of whispering to her. "Leslie Cairns," she answered before Jane could speak. "*Isn't that outrageous.* I want *you* to blow the whistle this instant. She's down there in the middle of a crowd. She won't be able to get free of it. She *must* be exposed Jane. It's necessary to the interest of the whole college that she should be sternly dealt with. Imagine her sneaking in here under the cover of a mask."

"Why—That *is* really dreadful, Julia," Jane whispered back. "Are you sure? Some of the freshies don't want the whistle blown until ten o'clock. The committee says it had better be after the next dance. I ought to do as they wish, you know. Where is she?"

"Down there." Julia nodded sulkily toward a group of enjoying wags at the far end of the gymnasium. Those who composed it were finding more sport in teasing Leslie than in dancing.

Marjorie was waiting until Julia should have finished whispering to the apricot mask before soliciting the latter's attention. She was uneasily watching the fun going on around Leslie. She could not be sure that the mask to whom Julia was whispering was the one to blow the unmasking whistle. For all she knew Julia might have stopped to cite her grievance to one of her particular friends.

"Is she that ridiculous, silly-faced mask?" Jane cried. "*She's* awfully droll."

"I fail to see it." Julia was haughtily contradictory. "Will you please blow the whistle now, Jane? You know she shouldn't be here."

"Please pardon me, I must speak to you." Marjorie had made up her mind to act. If the apricot mask were the soph detailed to blow the whistle, then she must be asked to delay blowing it until Leslie could be steered from the gym without discovery. If she were not the one appointed Marjorie decided that she would hurry down to Leslie and inform her of the danger.

"You have no—" Julia began angrily.

"I am Miss Dean," ignoring Julia, Marjorie serenely continued. "Will you please tell me who you are?"

"Yours truly, Jane Everest, Marjorie." A little laugh rippled out from behind the concealing mask.

"Oh, Jane!" There was inexpressible relief in the exclamation. "I'm so glad it's you. Are you the soph who is to blow the unmasking whistle? If you are, don't blow it for at least ten minutes yet."

"I insist that Miss Everest shall blow it, and at once," burst forth Julia Peyton furiously. "She has just promised *me* that she will."

"No, I haven't promised to blow the whistle at once, Julia," Jane steadily corrected.

"What right have *you* to interfere in our fun? Post graduates are not supposed to interest themselves too closely in class affairs." Julia tossed her head in withering disdain of Marjorie. "What right have *you* to prevent *me* from exposing that detestable Miss Cairns. Do you consider it honorable or fair to the traditions of Hamilton to permit a former student who was expelled to come on the campus socially?"

"How do you know, Miss Peyton, that Miss Cairns, a former student of Hamilton, is present in the gymnasium, or has been here this evening?" Marjorie inquired with a cool evenness that made Julia gasp. "Have you seen her?"

"I *know*, and so do you. Didn't she trip us with her umbrella? Didn't we hear her voice. *I* recognized it. *You* may not have." The answer was freighted with sarcasm.

"A masker carrying an umbrella tripped us. When she spoke her voice sounded like that of Miss Cairns," Marjorie stated impersonally. "I did not see the masker's face. Did you?"

"What difference does *that* make?" sharply countered Julia. "We both recognized her by her voice."

"Since we did not see her face how can we be sure that we recognized her. Lacking the evidence of our own eyes our best plan is to launch no accusations against Miss Cairns. Jane," Marjorie turned to the sophomore, "when are you going to blow the unmasking whistle?"

"After the next dance. This dance is ending now, I think." Jane turned momentary attention to the music, which was beating to a syncopated end. "That is the time the floor committee has set. I can change it if you like, Marjorie."

"No, thank you. That suits me nicely. I must go now, but I'll see you soon after unmasking, Jane." With a slight, courteous inclination of the head to Miss Peyton, Marjorie walked composedly down the great room to where Leslie stood, still surrounded.

Marjorie had not spoken to Leslie Cairns more than two or three times during the long period of time in which they had been students together at Hamilton. She had never spoken to Leslie since Leslie had been away from the college. She now wondered what she could say to the uninvited masker which might not be too humiliating to her.

CHAPTER XIII.

A FRIENDLY TURN

Circling the group around Leslie she approached the latter from the left side. Simultaneous with her approach the opening strains of a fox trot broke up the group. Not more than half a dozen persistent "rushers" lingered.

"Let's move on," she breathed to Leslie. She adopted a soft almost babyish tone. As she spoke she took light hold of Leslie's arm and began to steer her gently free of the few masks who were mischievously trying to detain the foolish-faced swain.

"Surest thing you know, sweetums," Leslie returned in a deep gruff voice. "You're the little kid who fell over my amberil. I didn't go for to trip you up, peaches. Want to dance?"

"Not yet. Let's go walking up the hall so folks can see your han'some face." Obeying an impish impulse Marjorie added, "It is simply celostrous. It's the only one you have, isn't it?"

"By cricky, it is. I ought to be proud of it." Leslie was oddly pleased to have the partner of "that screech owl" single her out for friendly attention. "I knowed you wasn't mad at me, kid," she next volunteered.

"No, I wasn't." The small soft voice held positiveness.

"That's fine. I *know* you've got a kind face." Both girls indulged in a smothered giggle at this inane tribute.

"Fade away," Leslie waved a careless hand toward two or three lingering tormentors. "Can't you let me and my girl alone?" She brandished her umbrella at them and swaggered out of their ken with Marjorie on an arm.

They looked after her, laughing, but did not pursue the pair. Leslie thought it extremely lucky that she should have been singled out for attention by "friendly ruffles." She had no idea where in the big room to look for Doris. She dared not linger to search for her. Her one thought now was to gain the safety of outdoors before unmasking time came.

Up the room the pair now strolled with an air of rustic gaiety. It was simulated by both with difficulty. They kept fairly close to the west wall of the gymnasium so as to be well out of the path of the dancers. Neither appeared to be in a hurry. Both were battling against a strong desire to break into a run.

They were nearing the door before a knowledge of what to say to Leslie came to little "friendly ruffles." Marjorie came into a sudden understanding that

Leslie was as anxious as she to reach the door. With unspoken intent both had steered directly for it.

Lightly withdrawing her fingers from her escort's arm Marjorie said in a very low, distinct tone. "The unmasking will take place after this dance. There will be a short intermission then. The girls will probably go parading about the campus."

"Who are you? Do you know me?" Leslie had instantly caught the hidden inference. Her partner knew her to be an outsider.

"Does it matter who we are? I must go. Good night." Followed the gracious addition. "Your costume was much the funniest at the romp."

In the second of silence which succeeded the compliment the two maskers faced each other, Leslie across the threshold now, Marjorie still inside the vestibule.

"Thank you, and double thank you," Leslie said in an odd muffled voice. "Good night." She turned and started across the campus at a swinging stride which might have belonged to a true country boy.

"Thank goodness," breathed Marjorie. She watched the lonely figure fast disappearing into the darkness and a feeling of pity rose in her heart because Leslie could not remain at the romp and enjoy the fun of winning the prize her ludicrous get-up merited.

It had taken longer than she thought to conduct Leslie to the door. Marjorie decided it to be hardly worth while to renew her search for Robin Page, whom thus far she had not been able to pick out among the rustic throng. She had not more than re-entered the ball room when the unmasking whistle blew shrilly. Its high, piercing blasts were immediately drowned by waves of echoing laughter as masks were removed and identities jubilantly made known.

Marjorie made a swift rush forward to meet an Irish country woman who was jogging peacefully along, a small, covered, green and white basket on her arm. She was dressed in a voluminous bright-figured brown cretonne dress. Over her shoulders was a green and red plaid shawl, on her head a white mob cap with a full white outstanding ruffle and a huge green satin bow decorating the front of it. Wide flat black slippers, green and red plaid hosiery which her ankle length dress permitted a glimpse of and a bright green umbrella completed her gay attire.

"Now for the sake av ould Ireland, is it yerself I am finding forninst me?" demanded the delighted Hibernian lady, offering Marjorie one end of her umbrella to shake instead of her hand.

"Yes, it is certainly myself and no other. But *where* have you been? Not out on the floor. I never saw sign of you in that costume until this minute. You tricky old Celt. You appeared late on purpose, *that's* what you did," Marjorie accused.

Leila smiled widely and cheerfully. "Now how can you blame me? Since I am Irish then how could I appear in the gym in an Irish costume of my own special fancy and not have the campus dwellers add two and two? So I have had a fine, exciting time sitting up in my room twirling my Irish thumbs until time for me to set out for the festival."

"What a mean thing to do; to put your friends to so much needless trouble. How long have you been on the floor?"

Leila looked thoughtful then beamed again: "Perhaps three minutes," she admitted. "I have not yet met a Traveler except you, Beauty. You are the same beauty-bright colleen as ever. You would be that though dressed in canvas bags."

"You are direct from County Blarney," Marjorie made a gesture of unbelief. "Jerry and I picked out Muriel first thing. She is so funny. I knew Ronny and Lucy, too, and Lillian. I'm sorry Kathie couldn't be in this. That's the penalty she pays for being of the faculty. Let's go Traveler hunting, Leila." She took Leila's arm and the two strolled on together further to investigate the many groups of mirthful, chattering rustics who crowded the spacious room.

It was not long before Leila and Marjorie were the center of a group of their own composed of Muriel, Vera, Lillian, Lucy, Barbara Severn, Ronny and Jerry. Leila circulated among them, beaming affably. She announced mysteriously that she had something nice to give each one.

"It's a gift basket which I stole from a leprechaun and in it is a magic charm for each and all. Be pleased to hold one hand behind your back when I give out the charms. Shut your fingers tight down on the charm so it can not vanish away. When I give the word you may look at them. Now be fair and do not peep at them until I give you the word."

With this glib injunction Leila slid a hand into the basket and drew it out tightly closed about some small object. She ordered the company to stand in a circle, each with a hand behind her back.

"What is it?" cried Muriel as her hand received and tightly clutched the small smooth round object.

"Now you shall see how fond I am of you." Leila had hurriedly given out the rest of the charms. "You may all look."

A chorus of derisive groans mingled with laughter followed the gracious permission. Each Traveler had been presented with a small potato. Its new pale skin had been scrubbed to immaculate cleanness.

"A charming charm, I must say," giggled Muriel. "Let's forcibly lead the Celtic sorceress out on the campus and peg at her with these praties. If she isn't hit by any of them we shall know that they are either bewitched or else we can't throw straight."

In the midst of the fun her friends were having over Leila's charms, remembrance of Leslie Cairns and her constrained flight from the scene of fun returned to Marjorie. She had sufficient cause to regard Leslie as an enemy, yet she did not hold her as such. Now she was feeling nothing but a kind regret that Leslie had barred herself out of Hamilton and all its pleasures. She decided that she would not tell even Jerry of the incident. Common sense whispered to her that Doris Monroe must have aided Leslie in the escapade. They had probably met on the campus and gone to the gymnasium together. Marjorie knit her brows in an effort to recall a dancing partner of Leslie's. She herself had noticed and repeatedly laughed at the foolish-faced farmer before the collision with Leslie.

"What are you scowling about?" Jerry happened to note Marjorie's puckered brows. "Let me sweeten your disposition by treating you to wintergreen lozenges and crimson lemonade."

"I accept your generous offer. I hope you have money enough to treat lavishly," Marjorie accepted Jerry with this pertinent hint, after having been affectionately jabbed in the side with Jerry's elbow.

"I got cash," Jerry boasted, thrusting her free hand into a pocket of her overalls. "I still got some 'o my Fourthy July money. I didn't spend nothing that day hardly. It rained lickety whoop. Silas Pratt near got swept off the speaker's stand a deliverin' his Fourthy July ration. I heerd at the last the stand floated right off in the woods a carryin' the Hamtown choir, Revern'd Skiggs and three boys as was sittn' on the bottom steps of it."

Marjorie and Jerry headed gaily for the lemonade stand calling back buoyant invitations to their friends to join them. As they drew near the stand a girl turned away from it and glanced at them. She was golden-haired and lovely in her white dimity frock scattered thickly with violets. Neither Marjorie nor Jerry could do other than admire her and her becoming costume. The trio did not exchange salutations.

Doris Monroe had not spoken to Jerry more than once or twice since coming to Hamilton. She had not even bowed to Marjorie since her own refusal to go to Sanford with Muriel on a Christmas vacation. Now she stared at

Marjorie's costume, rather than at Marjorie herself, in dismayed fascination. She had made a discovery which was anything but pleasing to her.

CHAPTER XIV.

A DISHEARTENING SITUATION

The discovery that Marjorie was the rustic maid in the pale yellow gingham gown who had accompanied Leslie Cairns to the door of the gymnasium was a distinct shock to Doris. Following the Rustic Romp she received a second jolt when Julia Peyton waylaid her on the campus to inform her triumphantly that she had something "very important to say about Miss Cairns."

"Whatever it may be, say it now," Doris commanded, keeping curiosity and interest well out of her tone. During the progression of her sophomore year she had grown to dislike Julia more and more. In the beginning she had tolerated resignedly Julia's jealous preference for her society. Now she did not care whether either Julia or Clara Carter liked her or not.

"I couldn't *think* of saying it now. I haven't time. It's something confidential." Julia crested her black head importantly. Her black, moon-like eyes fixed themselves upon Doris in a mysterious stare.

"Now, or not at all." Doris stood firm. "I'd prefer not to invite you to my room because of Miss Harding. I don't like to go to yours. You and Miss Carter nearly always quarrel. It's such a bore to listen to you." She affected a weary expression.

Julia cast a frowning glance about her. She glanced hastily up at the clock tower and said doggedly: "I must go. I'll meet you at the big green seat near the west side of the campus at five this afternoon. I have your welfare at heart, even though you don't think so," she flung this reproachfully at Doris. "I simply *must* speak to you about Miss Cairns."

Doris knew nothing of Julia's unfortunate fall over Leslie's umbrella. She had gone outdoors after a spirited dancing number, in company with half a dozen merry masks, for a breath of the sweet spring air. The spill had occurred while she was outside. When she had returned she had been immediately claimed for the next dance. A little later while dancing she had caught sight of Leslie surrounded by hilarious maskers. She had hurried to extricate her from her difficulties as soon as the dance was over. She had then spied Leslie moving towards the vestibule door in company with the mask in yellow gingham. It filled her with an immeasurable relief to know that Leslie had, as she supposed, escaped discovery and was then on her way to leaving the frolic.

To learn soon afterward that Marjorie Dean had been Leslie's companion to the door was not re-assuring. Her heart sank at the very thought until her first agitation had passed. She had recollected that, masked, Miss Dean might not have recognized Leslie. Leslie had promised not to talk. She and Marjorie were as strangers to each other; had been for some time. Doris could only marvel at the queer twist of fortune which had brought Leslie and Marjorie together. According to Leslie's accounts the two were bitter enemies. Masked, they had paraded up the gymnasium together on apparently congenial terms.

This latest thought completely re-assured Doris. Of course they had not recognized each other! Knowingly, neither would have gone a step with the other. Leslie had undoubtedly managed to free herself from her partner before reaching the door. Directly after the unmasking Doris had skipped a dance purposely to make a careful search on the floor for Leslie. Leslie had disappeared, completely and satisfactorily.

Doris had not said to Julia Peyton whether or not she would meet her at the big green campus bench near the west entrance. She changed her mind about going half a dozen times before five o'clock came. She had expected to hear from Leslie on the telephone through the day. No call from Leslie came until a quarter to five that afternoon. The message was a fairly polite invitation from Leslie to drive to Orchard Inn to dinner. She agreed to meet Doris on Hamilton Pike in front of the central campus gates.

Since she had come downstairs to answer the telephone Doris decided to walk over to the campus bench and learn what Julia had to say about Leslie. She was to meet Leslie at half past five. She would not spend more than ten or fifteen minutes in Julia's company. Since the romp was over, and nothing of mishap had occurred to Leslie on the frolicsome occasion, Doris was not inclined to borrow trouble over whatever Julia might have to say of Leslie.

"I'm glad you came." Julia rolled her black eyes at Doris in an expression of spiteful satisfaction. "You must have *some* idea of what I have to say, after what happened last night."

"I didn't intend to come. I happened to be downstairs, so I changed my mind about meeting you. I do not know what you mean by saying 'after what happened last night.' How can I possibly know what you are going to say?" Doris asked the question with a suspicion of sarcasm in her tone.

"Are you pretending you don't know what happened?" Julia asked offendedly. "Weren't you on the floor most of the time before the unmasking?"

"Yes, but I saw nothing happen, either remarkable or dreadful. You told me this morning you had something to say to me about Miss Cairns. Whatever happened last night has nothing to do with her," Doris said coldly.

"I don't understand you at all, Doris," Julia cried resentfully. "Didn't you know that Miss Cairns tripped Miss Dean and me last night while we were dancing, and that we both fell?"

Doris shook her head in blank amazement. "I did not know," she said very positively. "When did that happen? I went outdoors for a few minutes about two numbers before unmasking time. Was it then, I wonder?"

"Maybe it was. You admit then that Miss Cairns was in the gym," was the triumphant return.

"I admit nothing." Doris managed to keep up her cold composure. Anger gleamed in her green eyes.

"She was there, even if you won't admit it. She behaved like a boor to me. She crashed into us like a locomotive and poked a miserable umbrella she carried squarely between our feet. How could we help but fall? I simply said I thought it wasn't best for her to carry such a large umbrella on the dancing floor. You should have heard the insulting things she said to me, and to Miss Dean. She was in a terrible rage. I had all I could do to keep my temper." Julia endeavored to look very superior.

Doris did not make the mistake of uttering a word. She purposed to hear Julia out before speaking. The sophomore was more than satisfied to be allowed to do all the talking.

"I knew it was Miss Cairns by her voice. I was *so* shocked. After she had abused us both she swaggered off down the room. Then my partner told me that she was Miss Dean. I was *so* surprised. She said we had best not tell anyone just then that Miss Cairns was on the floor—the best way to do was not to mention names, but to order her out of the gym quietly. She did that very thing herself. Just before the unmasking I saw Miss Dean walking Miss Cairns up the gym and to the vestibule door. In two or three minutes Miss Dean came back alone." Julia gave out this information with malicious relish. "But that's not *all* Miss Dean did. She played a trick on the whole college which I think very ignoble." She paused to note the effect on Doris of this remarkable news.

"Go on," Doris commanded with bored amusement. "Your tale of the Rustic Mask is growing interesting."

"You may find it more so." A dull angry red overspread Julia's pasty-white complexion. "I haven't come to your part in it yet."

"No?" Doris smilingly tilted her golden head and raised polite brows.

"Miss Dean acted entirely against the traditions of Hamilton," she continued sullenly. "She went straight to Jane Everest, who was detailed to blow the whistle for unmasking and asked her not to blow it until she, Miss Dean, gave her the signal. She told Jane why, too. She had asked *me* not to say a word to a soul about Miss Cairns."

"How do you happen to know all this?" Doris asked in a quick sharp tone.

"I was with Miss Dean. I—er—I didn't—I couldn't get away from her just then. So I heard the whole thing." Julia floundered briefly, but ended in triumph.

"What did Miss Everest say?"

"She said she would wait to blow it. I was so disgusted with them both for their disloyalty to tradition I simply turned and left them. You know, Doris, that Miss Dean had no business to ask Jane Everest to disobey the order of the senior dance committee. They had set the time for unmasking. It was very dishonorable for her to try to shield an expelled student who had taken advantage of the masquerade to trick her way into the gym. Miss Cairns couldn't possibly ever again have hoped to take part in a college frolic after the way she left Hamilton. She was considered utterly lawless by the Board, Prexy and the faculty. I've heard *volumes* against her since I came to Hamilton."

"Miss Dean knows more against Miss Cairns, so I've been told, than any other student at Hamilton. She and Miss Cairns were rivals for popularity while Miss Cairns was on the campus. They used to play all sorts of dishonorable tricks upon each other, I suspect," Julia eyed Doris darkly, "that Miss Dean didn't have the—the—courage to expose Miss Cairns. It would take a person of very high principle to expose Miss Cairns openly on the floor of the gym, as she should have been exposed. I hope, for *your* sake, Miss Dean won't tell her pals about it. If she does, it will soon be campus gossip."

"Why for my sake?" Doris still refused to be included in Julia's implications.

"It's sweet in you to try to protect Miss Cairns, Doris, I honor you for it." Julia said, her reply reeking acidity. "But you can't deceive me. I know the farmer with the striped umbrella was Miss Cairns. I saw you go through the grand march and dance the first dance with her. I knew you by your walk and I came up close to you on purpose and took a good look at you to make sure. I know your emerald ring and I saw some of your hair fluffing out from under your hat."

"I went through the grand march and danced the first number with a rustic swain," Doris stated with deliberate coldness. "I did not see my partner's face. Did you?"

"That's not the point," Julia evaded, stung to exasperation by her classmate's cool reception of her revelation. "What I came here *specially* to tell you is that you had better not be seen going around with Miss Cairns. This story will travel, I feel sure. You'll be severely criticized and dropped by most of the students. Even your good looks won't save you. It was very inconsiderate and selfish of Miss Cairns to put you in such a risky position. She is certainly not your friend. The crowd last night was frisky. If the girls had had the least idea of whom she was they would have ripped off her mask, hooted her from the gym and maybe the campus. How would you have felt then?"

"I only know the way I feel now. I don't like you, Miss Peyton, and I never have." Doris chose to be drastically candid. "If a story such as you have just told me should go the round of the campus, I should not blame Miss Dean or Miss Everest for having started it. I should blame you. I intend to be silent. Let me give you a piece of advice. You had best be silent, too, about what you *believe* you know against Miss Cairns."

CHAPTER XV.

THE TRUTH ABOUT "BEAN"

Doris had only time enough to hurry back to the Hall for her wraps before starting out again to meet Leslie. She did not regret her blunt words to Julia. The gossiping, jealous sophomore had deserved them. Doris had grown tired of Julia's impudent interference into her personal affairs. This time Julia had gone too far. Doris had decided to drop her, oblivious of what the sophomore might afterward say of her. She believed sturdily that she could defend her own position at Hamilton.

"You certainly deserted me," was Leslie's greeting as Doris stepped into the roadster, parked at the central gates. "Last night, I mean," she added with her slow smile.

"I never meant to," Doris apologized. "You said you preferred to look out for yourself. I saw you in the middle of that crowd of freshies and was worried about you. By the time I could get free of my partner to go to you I saw you on the way out of the gym."

"Thanks to little yellow gingham ruffles, Leslie Adoree broke away from the merry rustic scene with colors flying and her false face still on. I had a good time, though, while it lasted."

"Did that unwieldy umbrella really trip a couple who were dancing?" Doris inquired abruptly. She was anxious to learn whether Julia had told her the truth in the matter.

"It really did." Leslie's face suddenly lost its half humorous expression. "One of them was a screech owl posing as a rustic youth. Her voice had a familiar sound. Still there are so many varieties of screech owl on the campus," she ended sarcastically.

"The 'screech owl' was Miss Peyton. The other girl was—"

"Miss Peyton. No wonder I felt like pitching in and fighting her while I had my farm togs on." Leslie's tone indicated her disgust. "She was outrageous, Goldie. I tried to stay dumb, but I couldn't. I finally said two or three pithy things to her. Little yellow gingham ruffles was all right. She tried to keep us from fussing. Afterward she came down to where I was and walked me away from a gang who had been trying to rag me. She walked me up the gym to the vestibule door and joked with me all the way. She had on a pale yellow gingham dress with little yellow ruffles and a white hat with—"

"What did she say to you, Leslie?" was Doris's anxious interruption. "I mean when you reached the door."

"That was the queer part. She knew me. I'm almost sure of it. She didn't say a word about my going, but she knew I wanted to get out of the gym before unmasking. She went to the door with me to keep off trouble. She was a good sport; an upper class girl probably. Some one I may have met. I know a few juniors and seniors who were freshies and sophs when I was a senior." Leslie gave an inaudible sigh. Last night's frolic had brought back vividly the memory of her failure as a student.

"The girl in the yellow gingham ruffled dress was Miss Dean," Doris said in a peculiar tone.

"What?" In her surprise Leslie allowed the roadster to run off the course on the pike she was keeping by several inches. She instantly brought the machine back to course. Apparently struck dumb, she leaned forward, staring interestedly at the road ahead. Just then she could think of nothing to say. Presently she found speech again.

"Yes, it was Bean," she said dully. "I know it now. Why didn't you come and walk me away from her when you saw us together?" Leslie demanded, her accent displeased.

"I didn't know then that the mask you were with was Miss Dean. I didn't know it until I saw her after the unmasking."

"She did me a good turn." Leslie stopped, her face reddening. It was the first time she had ever said a good word for Marjorie to any one. "How soon after I got away from the gym did the whistle blow?" she inquired soberly.

"Not more than two or three minutes. You got away just in time. I didn't know about Miss Peyton and Miss Dean and the umbrella business until this afternoon. Miss Peyton told me. I must have been outside the gym when it happened. I was out on the campus with a crowd for a few minutes."

Doris had wisely decided not to tell Leslie of what Julia Peyton had said. Julia was fond of telling her friends and classmates anything disagreeable which she might have heard of them. Doris abhorred the pernicious habit. Instead she began to quiz her companion about the umbrella mishap. She had a curiosity to know Julia Peyton's exact part in it. She had not wholly credited the sophomore's side of the story.

Leslie answered, at first rather abstractedly. Her mind was still centered on the "good turn" which "Bean" had done her. Presently she dropped into a humorous account of the accident which made Doris laugh. Julia had declared Leslie to be lawless and dishonorable. Doris wondered if it were really true of her. Leslie had treated her fairly. She began to believe she liked

Leslie despite the latter's occasional spells of domineering insolence. She made up her mind then and there to learn if she could the history of Leslie's and Marjorie Dean's enmity from its beginning.

Leslie's account of the umbrella incident, humorous and truthful, differed considerably from that of Julia Peyton. Doris wondered if Julia had not also misrepresented matters to her about Muriel at Christmas time. Then she remembered regretfully that Muriel had admitted having said the very things which had offended her pride. In the present instance she chose to believe Leslie rather than Julia.

"Miss Harding won the prize for having the funniest costume," Doris ended a little silent interval between the two girls. "She had on that ridiculous imitation of a riding costume. You remember we were laughing at her? The prize was a large jar of stick candy. Your costume was really funnier than hers. Your mask was so screamingly silly."

"Bean said I had the funniest costume," Leslie commented shortly. Her dark face grew darker as she sent the roadster speeding over the smooth pike. So it had been the girl she most disliked who had conducted her merrily and surely out of an embarrassing situation for which only herself was to blame. Her mind began suggesting petty spiteful reasons for Marjorie's kindly act. She dismissed them in the instant of their birth. None of them were honest.

Only one conclusion remained to be drawn in the matter. Leslie faced it unwillingly. To give it credence meant the crashing down of all the carefully built-up cases against "Bean" which she had cherished for over four years. In spite of the wilful and malicious attempts she had made against Marjorie's welfare and peace of mind, "Bean," it now appeared, had no grudge against her.

CHAPTER XVI.

THE JOURNAL

"That settles things for me, Jeremiah. For the first time since I entered Hamilton I'm not going home for the Easter vacation. General can't come home for a month from that Canadian trip. So Captain's coming here for Easter. Oh, joy! Tra, la, la, la, too, roo, re, lay!" Marjorie whisked up and down her's and Jerry's quarters at the Arms in frisky delight. A letter from her captain had furnished impetus for the dance.

"It's a good thing for us that Irma has changed the date of her wedding from Easter until the last week in June. That lets us completely out of going home. Not that I don't want to see the Macy family. I do; I do. But I must stick to you, Bean, till all is over. Then the Macys will have the pleasure of seeing Jeremiah for the rest of their lives. I feel a jingle beginning to sprout. Aha!" Jerry turned an imaginary crank on one side of her head and recited:

"Oh, let us sing, like anything,

And warble, too, re, lay.

No Feejee queen compares with Bean;

With Bean I choose to stay."

"You are a loyal Jeremiah as I've told you in the past, seven thousand times, more or less." Marjorie stopped her frisky prance to pat Jerry on the head. "Have you stopped to consider the feelings of the Macy family? They may strongly object to an Easter without Jeremiah."

"They'll have to bear it. It'll be the first long vacation for Jeremiah away from Macyville."

"And my first one away from Castle Dean. I promised Captain all the long Hamilton vacations before ever I entered college. I've kept my word. I would have this one, too," Marjorie declared earnestly. "Now Captain's coming to the Arms, and everything is more celostrous than ever."

"So it is, Bean; so it is," Jerry assured in what she liked to term her "most middle-aged, gentlemanly" voice.

"I should have felt like a shirker about going home at Easter. Leila, Vera, Robin, Ronny and Lucy say they can't spare the time away from the campus. It would have broken up my work on the biography a little, and I'd have hated to leave Miss Susanna. Still I would have gone. Captain first, you know." Marjorie lovingly patted her mother's letter.

"I'd have gone home with you and risked being called a shirker by the gang. I'd have borne it. I'm as noble as you are, noble Bean. Here is a copy of my latest jingle." Jerry tendered Marjorie a sheet of paper. "I caught it while you were busy praising me."

"Thoughtful bard," Marjorie commended, flourishingly accepting the paper. "May I inquire what you intend to do today?"

"I'm going over to the campus right after breakfast. Leila and I are going to make Norse helmets for Norse warriors of buckram and silver paper. With the help of our fertile brains and a little invincible glue we shall win. What are you going to do to while the day away?" Jerry inquired innocently.

"Oh, nothing special," Marjorie waved an airy hand. "That's the way it seems sometimes," she added, her face sobering, "when I write all day and then find at evening that I haven't done more than a page of good work. I've divided the material for the biography into two parts. I wish to call the first part 'Inspiration.' The second part will be 'Realization.'"

"It sounds good to me." Jerry waited breathlessly to hear more. It was the first time Marjorie had volunteered her any information on the subject of her own writing. Jerry watched her as she might have a rare song bird, which had poised itself near her and was ready to take flight at the tiniest movement on her part.

"'Inspiration' is to be the story of his youth, hopes and dreams. 'Realization' is to be the story of the man, Brooke Hamilton, and his achievement."

"Does Miss Susanna know what you've just told me? You have such clam-like tendencies, Bean." Jerry smirked at her chum.

"Yes, I told her about it several days ago. I only thought of it one day last week. I like the idea." Marjorie's accompanying smile was utterly without vanity. "If I could write as well as Kathie, or Leila, or you, Jeremiah, I'd be happy. Really, I have to dig out almost every sentence I write."

"Hooh!" derided Jerry. "I can't write. You're simply trying to be polite to present company. So deceitful!" She raised a hand in shocked reproach.

"I never allow anyone to call me deceitful." Marjorie charged upon Jerry, who nimbly eluded her and ran for the door. She whisked out into the hall and down the broad staircase with her vengeful pursuer close behind her.

The pair breezed around the corner of the newel post just in time to crash into Jonas, who was coming through the hall with a large feather duster which one of the maids had accidentally left on the hall rack.

"Mercy on us!" Jonas raised a startled arm. He poked the duster full into Jerry's face, to Marjorie's noisy delight.

"Ker-choo! I'm not the hall rack, Jonas, and I don't think I resemble the newel post, either," Jerry reproved.

"No, you don't quite look like either of 'em," Jonas agreed, chuckling. "Excuse me for dusting you," taking a leaf from Jerry's own book of etiquette he slyly added, "and blame yourself."

"Fine, Jonas, you're learning," Jerry heartily encouraged.

The frolicsome pair lingered in the hall for a little exchanging of merry repartee with Jonas. He now looked forward to such lively encounters as a part of his day's program.

At breakfast that morning Mrs. Dean's letter formed the main topic of conversation. Marjorie was bubbling over with happiness at the highly agreeable way in which her affairs had worked out.

"I'm the person fortune has singled out for attention," Miss Susanna crisply asserted. "All I need do is stay quietly at home and watch my friends gravitate to the Arms. Last Easter you girls all went away from Hamilton and left poor Susanna without a single playmate. This year Susanna has them all, and with one more to come from another land."

"It's wonderful to know that Captain will soon be here." Marjorie's voice was full of tender expectation. "Her presence will furnish me with oceans of fresh literary impetus. I shall need it for 'Realization,' the second part of the biography. It will be a good deal longer than the first part. I wish they might have been of equal length."

"The inspiration to build Hamilton College was his life. At least he made it that," Miss Susanna said rather absently. She appeared to be immersed in thought far remote from her spoken words.

"That's precisely why the first part of the biography will be so much shorter than the second," Marjorie cried, her forehead puckering in faint disapproval. "His very interesting years in China, the building of Hamilton, all his work belongs in 'Realization.' He had begun to work, then, you see, entirely toward realizing his splendid plans. I'd love to have more data about his youth. There is a great deal of the China data which would have been lost if you hadn't written down the stories he told you of his life in the Orient," she nodded gratefully to Miss Susanna.

"There may be some earlier data that I can let you have for that first part," was Miss Hamilton's vague promise. "I'll see what I can find for you."

Marjorie presently went to the study wondering not a little as to what the data might be which Miss Hamilton had promised. She surmised from the old lady's preoccupied air during the remainder of the meal that Miss Susanna was mentally trying to decide whether or not to give her for the biography certain incidents in the life of Brooke Hamilton which she had thus far withheld.

"I wish you could really speak and tell me something about yourself," she said fancifully to Brooke Hamilton's portrait. "What were your favorite sports when you were a very young man? Riding, of course, and probably swimming. Did you—let me think"—she stared reflectively at the portrait— "did you ever win a hundred yard dash, or—a yacht race?" She colored self-consciously at her own question. Her thoughts had veered suddenly from Brooke Hamilton to Hal Macy.

Thought of Hal next reminded her that she would not see Hal at Easter. That would be best for them both. Still she visualized Hal's disappointment, not only at not seeing her—he would miss Jerry's comradely companionship. It would be of no use to tell Jerry she ought to go to Sanford for Easter on Hal's account. Jerry would hoot at the idea. Marjorie decided that she would write Hal a particularly cordial Easter letter to try to make up for her absence.

She brought her mind summarily back to the subject of Brooke Hamilton. What was it Miss Susanna had once said of him concerning love? And when was it she had said it? An instant, and Marjorie recalled the occasion. It was the only time the mistress of the Arms had ever mentioned Brooke Hamilton as having loved. She had said on the occasion of Marjorie's introduction to the portrait of her kinsman in the study that Brooke Hamilton had believed in the romance of deeds; not the romance of love. She had also said that he had "found after all that love was love. That the romance of men and women—"

Miss Susanna had stopped at this juncture and had never again renewed the subject. Marjorie grew inwardly vexed with herself for having permitted her thoughts to run toward love. Because, unfortunately, Hal had fallen in love with her, the thought of Hal must ever bring reminder of the unwelcome fact. She was glad that Brooke Hamilton's history was one of deeds. In the mass of data she had handled there had been personal mention made of only his mother, Faith Gretney Hamilton, and Miss Susanna.

"I've been mooning," she informed the handsome, blue-eyed man in the gilt frame. "Now I am going to work hard. I must leave you in July for two whole months. I wish you would come down from the wall and finish writing your own story before I come back. Wouldn't that be a lovely magic surprise for Marjorie?"

A light tap on the study door sent her scurrying to open it. Miss Susanna walked into the study an odd look on her small shrewd features. In her hands she carried a rosewood box. It was perhaps eight by ten inches and not more than three inches deep. It was a lock box with a beautifully executed leaf border and a simple, artistically carved monogram on the shining surface of the lid.

"Marjorie, I have brought you Uncle Brooke's journal," Miss Susanna began without preamble. "I hadn't intended to let you or anyone else ever see it, much less permit a line of it to be published. Since you have been at the Arms I have wondered several times whether I was doing right in keeping it from you. How can you acquire a true conception of him unless you know him as his journal reveals him?"

As she talked Miss Susanna busied herself with the turning of a tiny key in the lock. She set the box on the study table, opened it. Inside it lay an oblong notebook bound in black leather. It was not very thick. Around it was a wide black rubber band.

"Here it is." The old lady lifted it from the box with a sadly reverent air; handed it to Marjorie. She accepted it, saying nothing. "It is a love story you are going to read in this old black book, Marvelous Manager; the love story of your friend, Brooke Hamilton. He was a marvelous manager, too, child. There was only one thing he did not know how to manage. That was his heart."

CHAPTER XVII.

BROOKE HAMILTON'S ANGELA

Marjorie looked from Miss Susanna to the portrait and back again. The mistress of the Arms was eyeing the portrait, too, with an expression of dark melancholy.

"There's no use in my staying here to talk with you about this journal, child. I've read it several times and almost cried my eyes out over it. In fact, I don't want to talk about it at all. I'm going. After you have read it, I'll have something else to say. Not until then."

"Thank you, Miss Susanna," Marjorie had only time to call after the sturdy little woman as the latter hurried from the room, furtively wiping her eyes with her hem-stitched handkerchief.

The young girl, who stood on the threshold of life and love, even as Brooke Hamilton had once stood, was equally the stranger to love that he had been. Marjorie regarded the black leather book with a glance of timid fascination. Between the loose black covers, broken apart from much handling, in that small space, was the record of a love which had not been a happy one. Over a happy love idyl Miss Susanna would never have "almost cried her eyes out."

She understood that her remark at the breakfast table concerning her lack of material for 'Inspiration' had set the question of the giving of the journal to her going again in Miss Susanna's mind. Marjorie felt as though she stood on the brink of the unknown. The love story of Brooke Hamilton could not but be different from that of any of which she had read or heard.

She swept aside the pad of paper on which she had been writing and carefully laid the journal on the table before her. Slowly she removed the wide rubber band and opened the book to the first page. There in his clear handwriting stood a foreword:

"May 1," it began. "This is my birthday, though not even the servants know it. Well, I have purchased myself a gift; this black book. It shall not be a black book in an evil sense. It shall only record my doings which I shall hope to make ever of purpose and right. Should I live to be a very old man this journal will preserve for me facts which memory will have long grown weary of holding. I shall call this book a present from my mother. I do not approve of making presents to myself."

Marjorie smiled at the final sentence of the foreword. It sounded so like Miss Susanna. The little preamble was distinctly boyish, she thought. It had the dignity, however, belonging to one brought up in loneliness.

She turned the page. The next item was brief and dated three years later, but again May 1, it stated:

"My birthday again. I found this book today in my desk. I had forgotten its use until I opened it. I shall try once more to keep a record of personal events. Three years between the two entries. How time passes."

To her surprise the next entry was dated July tenth, eight years later. It was humorously rueful.

"I appear to be most unsuccessful as a journalist. I have the will to record my doings but not the execution. Tonight I am in an oddly pleasant state of mind over the day's events. The Vernons, of Vernon Lodge, gave an archery meet this afternoon. They held the meet in honor of a cousin, Miss Angela Vernon, who has come to make her home with them. Miss Vernon is an orphan with a pleasing girlish face and soft chestnut curls. Her voice is low and sweet and she has a merry fashion of showing her small white teeth in laughing which is captivating. I enjoyed her company, which I cannot state to be the truth of the majority of young women whom I have met. I have no fault to find with these except that they seem to be possessed of so little depth. What a pretty name Angela is. I like it far better than Rachel, Maria, Abagail, Betsy or other feminine names similarly plain and ugly."

The Vernons' archery meet had staged the opening incidents in Brooke Hamilton's love affair. After the entry of July tenth, followed others, in somewhat scattered dating of the same year. Hardly one of these but that made mention of Angela Vernon. The young, attentive Brooke Hamilton had been horseback riding with Angela. He had escorted her to a lawn party. He had danced repeatedly with her at the Hamilton country-side ball. He wrote at some length in his journal of the pleasure he derived from her company. Yet into his writing never crept the word love.

Marjorie read on and on, forgetful of all but the world the journal conjured for her in which the author and Angela Vernon had once lived and played their parts. Thus far she had experienced no desire toward tears. Instead she was inclined to signal annoyance at Brooke Hamilton for his attitude of complacency toward charming Angela Vernon. At first she had been amused by his naive admissions to his journal, so utterly devoid of sentimentality. She had not then specially sympathized with Angela. From his written comments she could guess nothing of the young girl's mind toward him. An entry dated almost two years later than the fateful archery meet brought an odd aching sadness to Marjorie's heart.

"May 10. Life has moved very agreeably for me in my ancestral home during the years of my adolescence. Since my meeting with the Marquis de Lafayette, however, all within me is changed. There was a time to dance, to play, to be irresponsibly youthful. That time has past. I am facing the great problem of how one day to carry out my dream of founding a democratic college for young women in loving memory of my mother. In order to do this I shall require great riches. These I have not, though my father is not counted less than rich. I have a plan by which I may attain wealth in time. It must needs carry me far from home. So be it. I am a free spirit. I am bound by no pledge of love or duty.

"I am well satisfied that Angela and I are not more than friends. Sometimes I wonder if we are even such. She seems often cold, restrained in my presence where formerly she was invariably light and cordially gay. I confess I do not always understand young women. I shall soon be without her comradely company. She is going to Philadelphia to visit the Vernons there and dance at the Assembly Ball. She is very charming. She says she will never marry. Such a statement is not to be taken seriously. I have frequently assured her that she will no doubt wed a man high in the affairs of the United States. She is fitted for diplomatic society."

Followed other entries of a similar nature. Marjorie could not but marvel at the blindness of young Brooke Hamilton to Angela Vernon's love for him. Unversed in the ways of young women the very comments he wrote concerning her variable moods toward him Marjorie translated as the attempts of a girl in love to hide her unrequited affection from its indifferent object of worship.

Then came an entry made on shipboard on the day when the founder of Hamilton had embarked from New York on his first voyage to China. Her eyes misted with sudden tears as she read:

"Out at sea, the world before me! When I wonder shall I see the Arms again? Not, I am resolved until the battle's won, my fortune made, my dream become a reality. I have brought with me my black book, a link between me and my younger, lighter hours of life. 'When I became a man, I put away childish things.' So it is with me now. I must strive and accomplish in the world of deeds. Its only creed is action, and still more action. I shall keep my book now as the path back to youth's pleasant orchard.

"Angela gave me a utility case of dark blue silk which she herself made. She also gave me a small daguerrotype of herself. I was greatly touched by her remembrance of me. She rode down to the little station on her pony to wish me '*bon voyage*.' It was hardly more than dawn. Hers was the last face I saw among the home friends. She had been crying. She said so quite frankly. I had no idea she cared for me so fondly. She has flouted me roundly at times. God knows when we shall meet again. It appears strange that my friendliest comrade should have been a young woman rather than a young man. Angela has been such to me. I said to her in jest: 'You will have perhaps married and forgotten me, Angela, by the time I return to my country and the Arms.' She said: 'I shall never forget you, and I shall never marry.' So she thinks, but time creates many changes. I am weary of the pitching of the ship. I have not yet felt any indication of seasickness. I shall close you, black book, and seek my rest. You must be my comrade hereafter."

The part of the journal immediately following Brooke Hamilton's embarkation to the Orient continued with brief notes on the voyage. From that point on the entries dealt with the young fortune-seeker's life in China. These entries in themselves Marjorie found valuable as aids in completing the somewhat sparse data she already had regarding the young man's Oriental enterprise. Among them she found odd bits of Chinese wisdom which he quoted as the sayings of the several Chinese philosophers who had become his intimate friends. These original twists of mind, together with the numerous stories of her kinsman's life in China which Miss Susanna had dictated to her would beautifully round out the earlier chapters of "Realization."

Marjorie was presently surprised to find that the China entries covered a period of over ten years. Brooke Hamilton had evidently proved himself as irregular a journalist abroad as at home. While the entries were fuller than the earlier vaguer comments of youth, a year in time was often covered by three or four entries.

She read steadily through the record of commercial achievement which had brought him not only immense wealth but honor and distinction among a philosophical, far-seeing race rarely understood by Europeans or Americans. The Chinese had liked him for his truth and honesty. Because they had liked him they had helped him to his goal of attainment.

There was very little of Angela in this part of the record. Now and again her name would appear in, "I received a letter last week from Angela. It has been many weeks on the way to me, judging from the date of writing," or, "Angela writes that she believes I may never go back to America. How little a girl understands a man's high aspirations. My absence from home is merely a necessary part of my great plan. I shall try to make Angela understand. Hers is a fine mind. She should not lend it to such trivial conjectures. My return to America, God sparing my life, is certain."

Marjorie's sympathies were now firmly enlisted toward Angela. She marveled that a man possessed of Brooke Hamilton's fine spirit and high ideals should have so blindly passed by an unswerving devotion like Angela's. He had not loved her, and had been honestly unaware that she loved him. He had been too completely centered in the giant labor he had set himself to perform to stop by the way for flower gathering.

The last entry of the China group inspired Marjorie with somber consternation. It had been penned only a few months before the successful man of affairs had returned to America and Hamilton Arms.

"I nearly lost Angela, my little comrade." Followed a blank; as though the writer had paused in horror of his own words. "She has been near death of pneumonia. I am shocked beyond expression. I cannot image home without her to welcome me. Since receiving the bad news in a letter from her cousin, Adele Vernon, I have thought of Angela night and day. I shall leave my business interests here in Woo Fah's hands and sail on the next mail steamer. It is three months since Adele's letter was written. God knows what may have happened to my little girl."

Marjorie cast a sorrowful upward glance at the portrait. She thought she knew the tragic end of the blue-eyed man's love idyl. Nothing but the rustle of the notebook's leaf as she turned it broke the hush pervading the study. Her eyes met that which wrung from her a little cry of gladness.

"I have found love. I know its meaning now. I have come from the other side of the world to learn the wonder of all wonders. It is not the wonder of deeds. It is the wonder of a woman's love, changeless in its white glory. I walked in darkness, without knowing. Now I have come into the light. She always loved me, from the first day. How could I have been so blind? There was a woman, my mother, who loved me. There is a woman, Angela, who loves me now. I know only these two.

"We shall be married at Easter. That time seems far off. Angela tells me it is only five months away. From November until April I shall endeavor to lavish upon her the devotion she says she feared might never be hers. I chose achievement instead of love. Yet love did not forsake me. I have been magnificently favored by God."

The lovely, changeful face of the absorbed reader lightened a little over the cheerful turn in the story. Her faint smile died with the stark remembrance that Brooke Hamilton had not married. She continued reading with a sigh:

"Christmas Eve, eleven o'clock. I have just returned from Vernon Lodge. Early this evening I heard my favorite carol, 'God Rest You Merry Gentlemen' coming sweetly from the sitting room bow window. Angela, Adele and Bobby Vernon were the carolers. Angela's high, entrancing soprano voice still lingers in my ears. I think I shall never wish to hear a truer, sweeter voice singing the carol my mother so greatly loved.

"Of course I caught them, brought them into the house, kissed Angela's lips, under the mistletoe, kissed Adele's hand and shook hands with Bobby. I would have entertained them at the Arms but they marched me off to Vernon Lodge. There we had one more divinely happy evening together.

Angela is always so full of life, so brimming over with charm. I tell her sometimes she is too charming for her strength. She is rather frail still from the ravages of pneumonia. When we are married we shall go overseas on a long honeymoon voyage. This I believe will restore her to her former strength of constitution."

Marjorie hastily turned the leaf. She was prepared for disaster, but it came with a relentlessness which made her heart ache:

"May first. My birthday. I am alone. It is two months since Angela died. Is that a long, or a short space of time? I do not know. I know only she is gone. She complained of being weary in the evening. Next morning they found her asleep, her dear little crinkling smile on her lips. Pneumonia had weakened her heart. Even she did not know to what extent. This afternoon I gathered quantities of the double, fragrant purple violets for which the Arms has been famed since my grandmother's day. I took them all to the Vernon vault, my offering to love. Angela was not there, naturally. Her radiant spirit had long since transcended earth.

"I, Brooke Hamilton, a strong man, remain here. If only I had earlier understood love. I might have, had I not been so closely wrapped in my own dreams of achievement. What even greater things I might have accomplished with her by my side. Great love is the impetus to noble achievement. I know it now. Dear Angela! I bruised her tender heart with my selfish indifference to her love for me. God in mercy willed that I should not break it. Out of long years, four months! Forgive me, sweet. I shall never write in this book again."

Marjorie put her curly head down on the table and cried. She had lived and suffered that balmy spring morning with Brooke Hamilton. She had a sad impression that she had forever passed out of the comfortable state of disinterest with which she had formerly looked upon love. Nothing would ever be the same again.

CHAPTER XVIII.

ON THE ROAD TO ORCHARD INN

Mechanically, Marjorie closed the journal of Brooke Hamilton and slipped the rubber around it. She felt as though she never wished to open it again. What a tragedy lay between those black, worn, leather covers. Brooke Hamilton had suffered too greatly she thought for that which he was not really to blame.

He had not understood that Angela loved him. Still, he had upbraided himself with the remorseful thought that he might have understood, if he had tried. Angela had always loved him. She had known that she loved him. He had not in the beginning loved her, or at least he had given no thought to love. The last despairing entry in the journal held strong accusation against himself for not having given love a place in his life. Mind had dominated heart, when instead heart and mind should have gone seeking love and achievement together.

Then the thought which had been pounding at the walls of her brain for admittance entered her consciousness. Suppose that, some day, too late, she were to discover she really loved Hal? She had the same friendly regard for Hal which Brooke Hamilton had entertained for Angela. Hal loved her truly. Angela had truly loved Brooke Hamilton.

The mere idea of such a far-fetched catastrophe filled the sober-faced, lately tearful lieutenant with panic. She took the sad little history of a man's ambition and misunderstanding and hurriedly replaced it in the rosewood box. She turned the key, then placed the box in the cabinet. Having now read it, she could not bear to talk with Miss Susanna again about it that day. She longed to go out in the bright spring weather and walk until she had shaken off the deep-seated melancholy which had invaded her young heart. The quotation from Thanatopsis: "Go forth, under the open sky, and list to nature's teachings," recurred to her with force.

"It's almost time for luncheon," she murmured. "I can't help it. I must go outdoors for awhile. I shan't write a line today. Maybe not tomorrow. I'll scribble a note to Miss Susanna and give it to Jonas to hand to her. Jerry'll survive my desertion for once."

Luncheon at the Arms was at one o'clock. It lacked only a few minutes of one when Marjorie came downstairs to find Jonas and deliver her note into his hands. She had stopped only long enough to bathe her slightly pinkish eye-lids and draw on a pretty buff sports coat and hat.

She had hardly progressed the length of the long stone walk leading to the gate when her drooping spirits began to revive. She was not shallow, in that she could lightly throw off the impression of the morning's reading. She was strong-willed enough not to allow it to gain a distressing hold upon her. Most of all she wished to forget her dejected suppositions which concerned Hal.

Outside the gates of the Arms she paused to decide on which way to go. Should she walk to the town of Hamilton, or toward the campus. A walk into staid, drowsy Hamilton meant nothing more than a lonely prowling up and down the main streets. To go toward the campus! There was no telling who she might meet. Marjorie chose the campus, and variety.

"Now by King John's castle where may you be going?" Leila Harper called out the salutation as she swept past Marjorie in her car. A moment and it had stopped. Leila leaned far out of it, beckoning. "Have the feet to hurry," she ordered. "I have just been to town, but I'll take you back again in a trice, if you say."

"I don't want to go to town." Marjorie shook an emphatic head. "Take me for a spin, Leila Greatheart. I've quit biographing for the day and I wish to be amused; wish to be, and hope to be."

"I am that amusing! And you must have heard it. Now who told it to you?" Leila cocked her head to one side and smilingly awaited an answer.

"Leila Harper," laughed Marjorie. "I hope she knew what she was talking about."

"I hope so," Leila echoed fervently. "Let us take a ride, Beauty, to Orchard Inn. I should be busy with my Irish play this afternoon. I have no thoughts for it. We are both less gifted than we might be."

"Orchard Inn to luncheon sounds comforting." Marjorie was settling herself beside Leila in the car. "It's a glorious day for a drive. I've not seen you for more than a few minutes at a time since the Rustic Romp. I've only seen Robin once. She came over to the Arms the day after the Romp to tell me we made nearly a thousand dollars from it."

"Did you not hear, Beauty? Someone dropped a hundred dollar note into the cash box. Miss Dow had charge of the box. She had no idea who the generous rustic might be."

"Oh-h!" Marjorie's exclamation died in a soft breath. She had made a quick flashing guess as to the donor. Leslie Cairns, of course. What an odd proceeding on her part! Nevertheless Marjorie gave her the benefit of having been animated by a generous motive. She had undoubtedly come prepared to give such a sum. Marjorie was also of the opinion that Doris Monroe had paved the way for Leslie's lark.

"It is not a campus performance to give such wealth," smiled Leila. "I mean outside the Travelers and a few such princes as Gentleman Gus and her train of hearties. I thought Ronny might be the one. She accuses Vera; and so it goes."

"Whoever gave it must have wished her identity to be a secret." Marjorie would have liked to tell Leila of Leslie's lark. She had made up her mind that night, however, to be silent. Three persons besides herself knew it. No, only one, Doris Monroe. Jane Everest and Julia Peyton lacked the evidence of their own eyes. Unless Julia Peyton should gossip, Leslie's uninvited presence in the gymnasium would not be known.

"Since we have the gold, why should we seek the miner," Leila said genially. "'The Knight of the Northern Sun' is coming on grandly. Next Tuesday evening we shall give a full rehearsal. I trust our spear proof silver buckram helmets will fit our Norse warriors. Kathie is a true playwright, but I am a Celtic fake. It is hard to glorify my hero, since I am to be the hero myself. I am in a fine dilemma," she complained drolly. "Why did I ever imagine I could write an Irish play?"

It was an hour's run by automobile to Orchard Inn. It was the most distant from the campus of the coterie of tea rooms dear to the hearts of the Hamilton girls. The route lay for the most part over Hamilton Pike. The last three miles of the journey had to be made over a dirt road. It was fairly smooth and easily traveled except when roughened by heavy rains.

The two girls kept up a low steady stream of conversation as the car sped on toward the Inn. Both were feeling the pleasantness of a brief freedom from everything connected with even their beloved work. Neither had expected to take a trip to the Inn when she had started out. As a consequence, both were jubilant over the little excursion.

"Oh, I almost forgot to tell you something very important, Leila. We were so busy talking about the Travelers' stunts it almost slipped my mind. Captain's coming to the Arms for Easter." Marjorie's voice rang with joy. "That means I can stay here. Jerry is going to stay, too."

"May I ask whose marvelous managing that is?" Leila's eyes grew starry. She adored Mrs. Dean.

"Captain's. You see General will be away on a trip. Captain knows how much I have to do here, so she is going to help me by coming to the Arms. Miss Susanna is delighted. It's a case of Captain Bean making Lieutenant Bean and all the Beanstalks happy."

"We should start a Beanstalk colony here at Hamilton and remain here all our days. Would it not be a credit to the township and a satisfaction to my old age?"

"I'd love to live in Hamilton Estates, Leila," Marjorie confessed. "I care for Sanford because of Jerry, Muriel, Lucy and a few other chums of my high school days. If Jerry, Lucy, Muriel and a few more could be transplanted to Hamilton, I'd move Castle Dean here, too. Sanford has always meant a great deal to me. Hamilton means more."

"I understand. Midget and I have sometimes romanced of building ourselves a hut in the land of college." Leila looked dreamily away for an instant at the peaceful spring landscape. There was a touch of home hunger in her reply. She was silent for a little, her attention riveted on picking as smooth a route as was possible on the dirt road for the car. The machine had struck a rough, narrow stretch of ground not more than wide enough for two cars to pass each other.

"Hey, ho," she said, coming back to practicality; "I am not anxious to meet any cars on this cattle path." The words had scarcely left her lips when a low frame, black roadster, built for speed, appeared in sight upon the brow of an incline ahead of them. "Do you see that, Beauty? I had but to speak when a listening jinxie whisked a black hob-goblin into my path," Leila cried out in mild vexation.

Marjorie watched the approaching car with more than casual interest. A comprehensive glance at it had informed her as to the identity of the driver. A young woman was at the wheel, the car's sole occupant. Marjorie did not miss seeing the peculiar expression which showed itself in the other's face as she glanced at Leila's car and prepared to keep strictly to the proper side of the narrow road.

Instead of starting down the low hill the other motorist stopped her car at the top of the little rise of ground and waited for Leila's roadster to come up. As Leila's car came abreast of her automobile she leaned out and cried: "Will you please stop your car? I'd like to speak to Miss Dean."

"Has the world come to an end?" Leila muttered in Marjorie's ear as she complied with the other girl's request. "The Hob-goblin is no myth, as you can see for yourself, Beauty."

CHAPTER XIX.

I'M SORRY

With Leila's muttered comments in her ears Marjorie had hard work to keep a sober face and maintain an air of pleasant impersonality toward Leslie Cairns. She could think of no reason why Leslie Cairns should speak to her. She thought Leslie could hardly have guessed her identity since the Romp. Certainly on that night Leslie had not recognized her. The fact that she had amiably permitted Marjorie to conduct her to the door and freedom was sufficient proof in itself.

"Good afternoon, Miss Dean." Leslie's salutation was laconic. Marjorie thought she was looking particularly well in a sports suit and hat of bright brown English weave. Her irregular, dark features bore no trace of ill humor. Instead her face was singularly impassive.

"Good afternoon, Miss Cairns." Marjorie's clear brown eyes looked straight into Leslie's small black ones. She could think of nothing to say. She therefore waited for Leslie to make the next advance in conversation.

"It's about the other night, I'd like to speak to you," Leslie declared with somber steadiness.

"Pardon me. I am willing to listen to whatever you may wish to say to me, Miss Cairns, but—I am with Miss Harper," Marjorie reminded with candid courtesy.

"Miss Harper is welcome to hear what I have to say to you. She probably knows already that I—"

"She knows nothing of—of—certain things from me. Pardon me for interrupting you." Marjorie smiled friendly warning.

"I am sure she doesn't," Leslie agreed with an odd energy which brought a faint flush of surprise to Marjorie's cheeks. "She must have heard it somewhere on the campus, though. I thought possibly that screech owl—I'll say Miss Peyton, one's her natural name, the other only a surname, had published me on the main bulletin board before this." Mention of Julia Peyton filled Leslie's tones with contemptuous sarcasm.

"Hardly." The quick sturdiness of the retort brought a peculiar gleam to Leslie's eyes.

"It was a mistake—losing my temper as I did." Leslie's next speech came with shamed apology. "I don't know that it matters specially—now. The mischief's done. I had no business in the gym that night." She looked at Marjorie as though asking for an opinion.

Leila sat the picture of immobility. Her hands loosely clasped the wheel. Her blue eyes stared straight ahead. She affected deep interest in the immediate road ahead of the car. She had had no inkling of what Leslie meant until the latter had made pertinent allusion to the gymnasium. Light had then broken upon her acute Irish intelligence. Comprehension threatened to break up her immobile expression.

"That is of course true from—from a certain standpoint," Marjorie admitted. "If you wish my personal opinion," she smiled; "I can't see but that your presence there was an added attraction to the crowd. I have fought for democracy at Hamilton, Miss Cairns. I can only feel my attitude to be democratic now. I believe that you went to the Romp merely to have fun. There could be no harm in such a motive."

"There wasn't!" Leslie cried in sharply anxious agreement. "I had grown tired of myself and only wanted to have a good time. I wouldn't do such a stunt, again, though. I'm through with such performances. I'm through with everything," she added with a dull kind of desperation.

"I think I understand how you felt about going to the Romp," Marjorie said gently.

"Still you wouldn't have done so. That's the difference between your disposition and mine. Never mind about that. I've just one thing to tell you. I wish you'd believe me. I'm all through trying to make trouble for you at Hamilton or any place else." Leslie's earnestness was unmistakable.

"It—truly, Miss Cairns, it doesn't make—" Marjorie colored with growing confusion.

"Oh, but it does. I want you to know, Bean—" It was Leslie who now turned very red. Before she could offer an abashed apology Marjorie's merry laugh rang out.

"Please don't." She gaily warded off apology. "You can't imagine how truly fond I've become of being called 'Bean.' It's funniest of two or three pet names the girls have given me. Miss Macy has even composed some funny verses which she calls 'Jingles to Bean.'"

"What?" A slow smile succeeded Leslie's momentary air of uncertainty as to whether she had heard aright.

"You have a keen sense of humor, Miss Cairns," Marjorie generously continued. "Your costume the other night showed your appreciation of funny things. You spoke of Miss Peyton. She was unfair with you at the dance. I was glad you walked away from her, and sorry that you should have been aggravated by her to the point of answering." Marjorie tried to lead the subject away from intimate personalities. She disliked to make apologies. She disliked far more to receive them. She desired no promise of future rectitude from Leslie.

"Leila," she addressed Leila's clear-cut Irish profile, "have you heard that Miss Cairns was masked at the Romp?"

"I have not." Leila slowly turned her face toward Leslie. "May I inquire what your costume was? I was not in the gym until a very few minutes before the unmasking," she explained.

"I was just a farmer, blue overalls, gingham shirt and all that sort of thing," Leslie described briefly. "I happened to get hold of a particularly silly-looking mask. That was the funny part of the costume."

"And now I will tell you the funny part of your adventure." Leila regarded the girl she had ranked as her pet aversion with a not unkindly glance. "I have heard nothing about you in connection with this funny-face farmer, but I have heard plenty of myself. It seems I had the credit for being that one. I was not on the floor while you were. I waited in my room so as to tease the girls. I had bet with a crowd of freshies that none of them could pick me out in that rustic mob."

"Why, that,—" Marjorie began.

"Is why there was a crowd at my heels all the time," finished Leslie rather excitedly. She and Marjorie both laughed.

Even Leila's austerity of feature relaxed into an amused smile. "I must have come into the gym when you were preparing to leave it for I caught not even a glimpse of such a costume as you had. Now a rumor is drifting merrily about the campus that I was the funny mask, but that I changed to an Irish peasant costume to puzzle the freshies."

"How utterly providential!" Marjorie's opinion was cordially hearty. "I am afraid I shall be too busy from now on to enlighten the campus dwellers concerning their fond delusion."

"I have plenty to do myself," was Leila's vague inference.

Leslie's eyes traveled from one to the other of the pair of amused faces. Were these the two Hamilton girls she had hated so unreasonably when a student in college with them? She now dejectedly wondered why she had hated them.

"There's something I must say to you," she persisted to Marjorie. "I used to hate you. That is, I thought I hated you. After I found out who you were I knew I could never hate you any more. You took with you all my weapons of offense. Why should I ever have hated you? The answer goes back to myself. You ought to hate me. But I know you don't. That makes me double hate myself." Leslie made an impatient movement of the head, indicating her distaste for herself.

"I never hated you, Miss Cairns. I've felt dreadfully exasperated with you at times," Marjorie honestly admitted. "I haven't felt that way toward you for a long time," she added with her winsome smile.

"That's good news." Leslie faintly answered the smile. Her hands began to tighten on the wheel. "Oh, yes, I almost forgot. Miss Monroe had nothing to do with my campus lark. I planned it myself. She knew of it, but it wouldn't be fair to censure her for what I would have done anyway. Will you stand by her if—if any gossip should start about the affair?" Leslie looked almost appealingly from one to the other of the two Travelers.

"You need have no fears in that respect," Marjorie promised staunchly.

"There will be little or nothing said," was Leila's dryly authoritative prediction.

"Thank you both. That's all, I believe, except—I'm sorry. I'm saying it, though about five years too late," Leslie declared bitterly.

Marjorie made no verbal reply. She bent upon Leslie a glance brimming with toleration. Its frank kindness made Leslie feel like bursting into tears. Pride alone kept her from it.

After a moment Marjorie said: "We have something to thank you for, Miss Cairns; the hundred dollar note you dropped into the money box the evening of the Romp. We understand and appreciate the spirit that prompted the gift. When I say we, I mean the Travelers."

Marjorie made the assumption boldly, hoping thus to take Leslie unawares. She succeeded. Leslie colored hotly. Hastily she started the motor. "Good-bye." She smiled a queer, wry smile; nodded first to Leila, then to Marjorie. Next instant her car had passed theirs and was speeding away from them.

CHAPTER XX.

BEGINNING TO GROW UP

"Can that be Leslie Cairns?" marveled Leila. "You will now kindly tell me a great many facts about her recent history which I have somehow missed. You intended to tell me about them, did you not?" She regarded Marjorie with laughing suspicion.

"I had not intended to tell you or anyone else that she attended the Romp," Marjorie said emphatically. "I never even mentioned it to Jerry. You see what a good secret keeper I am. Since you have heard a part of the story from the heroine herself, I may as well tell you the rest."

"Leslie Cairns's wits are as ready as Jerry's when it come to giving out names," was Leila's comment after Marjorie had informed her of the set of circumstance at the Romp in which Leslie had so prominently figured. "Jerry and Muriel named Miss Peyton the Prime Minister. That was appropriate enough last fall when she tried so earnestly to dictate a policy of her own to we poor timid P. G.'s. It seems she has practiced screeching as well as dictating. And she looks like an owl!" Leila's intonation was full of false enthusiasm.

"I made up my mind not to tell Miss Cairns about Miss Peyton and Jane Everest. It wasn't necessary. She is worried now for fear Miss Monroe may be blamed. It seems odd, Leila, that Leslie Cairns should have shown consideration for another. I say it candidly; not spitefully. She ought to be protected if only for that change toward growth." Marjorie was very earnest in her conviction regarding Leslie.

"It is a nine days' wonder to me." Leila was impressed in spite of her earlier impulse to be skeptical. "If nothing is brought up against Leslie Cairns now on the campus, nothing will be later. The time of interest for a rumor is just before, at the time, or just after something supposedly happens. The Romp is now almost a memory. Soon along will come something new and amusing to crowd that memory out."

"There is still the other side of it, Leila." Marjorie grew grave. "It was against good taste in Leslie Cairns to step into the social side of Hamilton College under cover of a mask. She had forfeited the right to do so when she left Hamilton two years ago."

"Still it is the most harmless piece of mischief that she ever carried out. And she dragged no one else into it," Leila said thoughtfully.

"Precisely the point, Leila. I've felt so about it ever since I went to the door of the gym with her that night." Marjorie spoke her mind forcefully. "I couldn't regard her lark as anything but a lark. Her costume was so funny and she behaved in such a funny, original way. She was more like a child than a young woman. It was as if she had slipped through the gate of a high fence, and into a forbidden yard. She acted as if she were having a fine time playing. Perhaps she went over a rustic road to childhood that night, and when she came back found herself changed?" Marjorie made fanciful suggestion.

"It may be so. All the fairy tales are not hatched in the Emerald Isle." Leila cast a sly smile toward her fanciful chum. "More's the pity that I instead of she should be given credit for her costume. For that I shall see to it that she gains in another direction. Ah-h-h!" Leila gave the wheel an inspired jerk which sent the car bumping into a rut. "I have just thought of a plan to keep the Screech Owl from screeching on the campus."

"Have you? I'm glad to hear it." There was a hint of grim enthusiasm in the reply. "What will you do?"

"I shall have to try it out on her first and tell you my method afterward. It is only the ghost of a plan yet." Leila made evasive answer.

Marjorie did not inquire further into Leila's "ghost" of a plan. "All right. Keep it to yourself. I only hope it will be effective. It's hard to believe, isn't it, that we should be planning now to protect Leslie Cairns? When one stops to remember that she—"

"Never did anything but harass and torment us," supplied Leila, "it is that amazin'." Her accent became strongly Hibernian.

"That's not quite what I meant to say, but it's true. We can afford to be generous to her, Leila."

"Ah, yes. It is more becoming to old age," sighed Leila, then chuckled. "As ancient, tottering P. G.'s we are so merciful!"

"That's one explanation. It will do as well as another," laughed Marjorie.

"We have an old Irish saw that runs: 'What is the gain in beating a knave after the hangman has him?'" Leila lightly quoted the quaint Celtic inquiry.

"What is the use? That is exactly the question," Marjorie smiled in sympathy with the pertinent old query. "Leslie Cairns has made things far harder for herself than for us."

The two girls fell silent after Marjorie's remark. Both were thinking of the past five years in which Leslie Cairns had figured so unpleasantly. Neither cared to continue the conversation with Leslie as the chief topic. The lure of Spring had chained them both to dreamy admiration of her budding beauty.

The automobile had swung into the last lap of the road to Orchard Inn which wound in and out like a pale brown ribbon among orchard belts of fragrant pink and white bloom. Orchard Inn itself to which they would presently come, was a staunch brick relic of colony days, set down in the midst of thick-trunked, gnarled apple trees. Just then they were burgeoning in rose and snow, scented with Spring's own perfume.

Marjorie had always been a devoted worshipper at the shrine of Spring. The glorious resurrection each year of earth, which had lain stark and drear under winter's death-like cloak, seemed to her the mystery of mysteries. Today the very sight of brown fields turning to emerald, apple, pear and cherry trees rioting in ravishing bloom, the twitter of nesting birds, busy putting the last touches to their tiny homes, filled her with retrospection. Sight of a peach tree, a luxuriant bouquet of vivid pink gave her a sensation of unutterable sadness.

She understood dimly that her mood of wistful sadness was born of more than her ardent love of Spring. She was still gripped by the supreme tragedy of Brooke Hamilton's love story. She almost wished she had not read it. She was sure that she could never bear to read it over again. In the next breath she made sturdy resolve that she would. She would not allow herself to be affected to such an extent even by a story as sad as was Brooke Hamilton's.

Then, without invitation, Hal invaded her thoughts. She was no nearer being in love with him than she had ever been, she reflected with an almost naughty satisfaction. Nevertheless, the moment she began to think about love, he appeared, a blue-eyed image of her mind, always regarding her in the same sorrowful way, in which she had caught him viewing the portrait of the "Violet Girl."

Marjorie had no suspicion that she had changed a great deal in mind since the evening at Severn Beach when she and Hal had walked together with their friends along the moonlit sands and Constance had sung "Across the Years." She had listened to the sadly beautiful song, which had breathed of blighted hopes and love's misunderstandings without either sentimentality or sentiment of mind. Hal had characterized her faithfully when he had told her that she had not yet grown up.

Neither he nor she knew that the growing-up miracle had begun when she had laid her childishly curly head on the study table and cried out her heart over Brooke Hamilton's tragic love affair.

CHAPTER XXI.

THE MEETING

While Marjorie and Leila rode on through fragrant spring bloom to Orchard Inn, Leslie Cairns drove slowly toward the town of Hamilton. She was filled with many emotions, but the chief one was that of surprise at the way in which she had been received by "Bean" and Leila Harper. She had always stood a trifle in awe of Leila and her cleverness when the two had been classmates though she had affected to despise the gifted Irish girl. Marjorie she had hated from the first meeting. Or thus she had narrowly believed until she had come into the knowledge that "little friend ruffles" and Marjorie were one and the same. She had also come into a knowledge of Marjorie which she could not ever again overlook.

A friendly act on Marjorie's part, the prompting of a broad tolerant spirit had been the magic which had worked a well-nigh unbelievable change in Leslie. It is often the small, seemingly unimportant happenings in life which frequently are instrumental in working the most amazing transformations.

While Marjorie was going through one process of growing up Leslie was going through another widely different phase of the same process. Leslie had begun to learn that: "He who breaks, pays." Until her garage failure she had been childishly stubborn in her belief that she could successfully "get away with" whatever she undertook to accomplish. She had suffered untold mortification of spirit over the ignominious end her father had put to her business venture. She had read and re-read the letter which her father had at that time written her until she knew every scathing word of it by heart. This in itself had produced a beneficial effect upon Leslie's wayward character. In time to come she would regard that particular letter as the turning point in her life.

The downfall of her business hopes had furnished her with gloomy retrospection for long days after she had returned to New York. With all the fancied grudges she had against Marjorie she was obliged to admit to herself that "Bean" had certainly not been responsible for her father's unexpected visit to Hamilton. Neither was she to know until years afterward that a "Bean-inspired" advocate of justice in the person of Signor Guiseppe Baretti had proven her business Waterloo.

Sullenly obeying her father's stern command to renew her intimacy with Natalie Weyman, Leslie had reluctantly got into touch again with Natalie. Natalie, however, was betrothed to a young English baronet. She was consequently interested in nothing but herself, her fiancé and an elaborate trousseau of which she was imperiously directing the preparation.

Leslie felt utterly "out of it" at Nat's playhouse. She lounged in and out of the Weyman's imposing Long Island palace with the enthusiasm of a wooden Indian. She listened in morose silence to Natalie's fulsome eulogies upon her fiancé, Lord Kenneth Hawtrey, the Hawtrey ancestral tree, her own trousseau and the two-million dollar settlement her father proposed to make over to her as a bridal gift. Leslie mentally tabulated each of these fond topics upon her bored brain and learned to know by the signs just when each of them would be complacently brought forward by her former college chum.

When she could stand the strain no longer she had announced to Mrs. Gaylord that her father had gone to Europe and that she intended to buy a new roadster and drive to Hamilton. "You can stay here or go along, Gaylord. Suit yourself. My advice to you is to stick to me. Peter the Great will approve of such devotion on your part. He knows I'd go, even if you were to try to squash the expedition. Your part is 'Never desert Leslie,'" was the succinct counsel she gave her chaperon.

While Leslie was engaged in driving slowly toward Hamilton wrapped in her own half sad, half relieved mixture of thoughts, a tall man in a leather motor coat and cap ran down the steps of the Hamilton House and sprang into a rakish-looking racing car parked in front of the hotel. His heavy dark brows were corrugated in a frown. His lips though firmly set harbored a grim smile.

He had driven through the sunny streets of sedate Hamilton that afternoon as one who knew the place but had been long away from it. This was his second call at the hotel. On both occasions he had seen and talked with Mrs. Gaylord. His business, beyond a few, dry unreproving sentences, was with Leslie Cairns. As Leslie confidently believed him to be in Europe she was scheduled to receive a decided shock.

Peter Cairns, for the man in the racer was he, was soon speeding over Hamilton Pike, through Hamilton estates and on past the college wall toward a squat stone building which had the appearance of an old-time inn. In front of it he parked the racer again and strode up the long stone walk toward the quaint low door with its swinging wrought iron lamp.

Within the restaurant Signor Guiseppe Baretti was in earnest consultation with his manager. He glanced up at the newcomer, who, instead of choosing a table and making for it, headed directly for him. That the little, shrewd-eyed proprietor of the restaurant and the broad-shouldered financier had a bond in common was plainly evident from the way in which they shook hands at the close of the financier's short call.

"What you think? What you think?" the Italian excitedly demanded, catching his manager's arm as the door closed behind his caller. "This is the father the girl we write the letter about. When he comes here, just now, a little while, he says to me: 'How'r you? You don't know me. I am Peter Car-rins.' I think this mebbe where I get the hard beat, cause I have tol' this man what trouble his daughter make Miss Page, Miss Dean. But this is what say: 'I am to thank you for your letter. I have not the time today talk much with you. Before long I come here again. Then I tell you som'thin' su'prise you verra much.'

"I say then to him I think he come to give me the good beat for my letter. He laugh. He say: 'No, no.' Put up his hand like that." Baretti illustrated. "'I un'erstand you verra well. I have been much in Italy. I know the Italiano.' Then he speak me good Italiano. Now that is the father Miss Car-rins. What you think? She is here in Hamilton again. Mebbe her father don' know it. I believ' he don'. Mebbe she don' know he is here. When both find out, then oo-oo, much fuss I guess. Mebbe Miss Car-rins get a good beat," he predicted with a hard-hearted chuckle.

If he had walked to the door after Peter Cairns instead of lingering to acquaint his faithful little countryman with the identity of the stranger, he would have seen something interesting. He would have seen a trim-lined black roadster slow down to a sudden stop as the result of a peremptory hail from a racing car which had drawn up alongside. In short, Baretti would have seen Leslie Cairns and Peter Cairns meet precisely in front of the east-end gates of the campus.

CHAPTER XXII.

A BUSINESS PROPOSAL

"Run your car off to one side where it won't interfere with the traffic." The financier ordered Leslie about precisely as he might have ordered one of his men. His tones reached her, coldly concise, entirely devoid of affection. "There, that will do." He skillfully manipulated the racer to a point parallel with her car, but out of the way of passing automobiles.

"What do you want?" Leslie inquired with sulky coolness.

"What are you doing here?" sternly countered her father.

"Nothing. You took away my job."

"A good thing I did. I ordered you to stay in New York. Why are you not there? Why didn't you obey me? You're courting business college, it would seem."

"Things are not always what they seem," Leslie came back laconically.

The financier set his lips anew. It was either that or smile. Leslie was regarding him with the curiously unafraid expression which had most amused him in her as a child.

"Why can't you behave properly?" he demanded with vexed displeasure.

"I don't know. I have been trying to find that out for myself lately. It's a hard job, Peter." She purposely called him Peter. It had been another of her laughable childish mannerisms.

It brought a smile, reluctant and fleeting to his face. An odd light burned in his eyes for an instant. He turned his head to avoid her penetrating gaze. He had never before heard Leslie make an allusion to self-analysis. The knowledge that she had begun to try to fathom her forward motives was encouraging.

"What mischief have you done since you came up here?" he next asked. "Why could not you have cultivated Natalie instead of racing over the country up here in a car?"

"Nat is going to be married to a monocle and an English title. She is hopeless. I couldn't stand her. I fled to the country, Peter. I knew you wouldn't wish to have me die of being bored. Don't rag Gaylord for it. I made her come here. She's a good, ladylike sport, who knows how to stick to me and yet mind her own affairs. You may think you picked her for me. No, no; I saw her first. That gives me a prior claim to bossing her. I'm glad I met you, if only to settle that little point in your mind." Leslie's hands busied themselves with the wheel. "I think I'll go on," she declared tranquilly. "Don't worry, Peter, I won't do anything more to disgrace you. I'm going to lead a noble life from now on."

She was fighting desperately to maintain humorous indifference. It was the side of her character which Peter Cairns most appreciated. She was now fighting to regain the proud interest he had once taken in her ready wit and irresistible humor. Her reprehensible behavior had amounted to stupidity. Peter Cairns most hated stupidity in man or woman.

Peter Cairns repressed an audible chuckle at this latest news from his lawless daughter. "This is not the place to discuss ethics," he said dryly. "Run your car into town and meet me in the hotel lounge."

"Race you in; cross town, or any old way?" Leslie proposed on impulse. She eyed her father doubtfully.

For a long moment the two stared into each other's faces, as though each were endeavoring to determine the strength or weakness of the other.

"I'll go you." Peter Cairns spoke with a finality which set Leslie's heart to pounding violently.

"My car was built for speed and I know how to get the speed out of it without arousing the natives. Look out, and don't get pinched." Leslie brought her car up on an exact line with the racer. "One, two, three, go to it," she called animatedly. Then she was off over the pike on not only a go-as-you please race to Hamilton. She was on the first lap of what she hoped would be the quick road back to her father's heart.

Leslie won the race. Peter Cairns was not familiar with the short cut she took. It bumped her car over a stretch of uneven paved street but brought her triumphantly to the entrance of the Hamilton House at least a minute ahead of her father's car.

"Why did you pick Hamilton of all places to come back to?" Peter Cairns was presently demanding of her. The two had seated themselves opposite each other in a deserted corner of the lounge.

"Probably the scene of my many crimes held a fascination for me," Leslie advanced with a reflective air that completely upset the financier's hitherto carefully preserved gravity. He laughed outright.

"What did this Miss Dean against whom I understand you had so much spite ever do to you that was unfair or dishonorable?" His alert features had quickly returned to their customary aloof cast.

"Not a blamed thing, Peter," she said in a tone of sober humiliation. "You were right. I am several kinds of idiot, bound in one volume. The war's over. I surrendered this afternoon, just before I met you. Whatever you know about Bean and me is probably true."

"Who is Bean?" demanded Peter Cairns.

Leslie enlightened him. At the same time she quoted Marjorie's own recent remarks on the subject. "You can see from that why I quit," she said. "There was nothing else to do. Some day, when I've really put over a good square business enterprise I'll tell you the story of Bean, her Beanstalks and Leslie Adoree."

"Your first business ought to be to repair the mischief you made," was the severely judicial response. "Unfortunately you can't undo the anxious, troubled hours which your malice has imposed upon others. You have taught me a lesson. I needed it. My code of finance has been that of a hawk. I have revised it on more humane lines. I'd rather not have learned it from your mistakes. But it's been learned now. I am not sorry I cut you off from me. Perhaps it was not the way to do. I don't know. I loved you very tenderly as a child, Leslie. I was proud of you as a youngster. I should like to be proud of you as a young woman. What are the prospects?"

"Good, Peter. The best since the days when I was your pal and we planned to conquer the universe together. I'm trying to think of a way to make amends." She met her father's measuring glance with an air of patience quite foreign to her old wayward self. "I like it up here. I've a girl friend on the campus. I really like her. I want you to meet her. Gaylord approves of her. What more can you ask?"

"I'll take you at your word." For the first time since meeting her father he held out his hand. Leslie placed her right hand in his strong fingers. Her left reached out very timidly and covered the hand she held. It was the silent ratification of affection between Peter and Peter Cairns' daughter.

"How did you know I was here?" she asked after a brief silence.

"I told Wilkins, my secretary, to keep track of you. I made only a flying trip to Europe. He told me you were here. I drove here soon after leaving the steamer. I had business at Hamilton Estates."

"What are you going to do with my garage flivver?" A gleam of intense curiosity lived in Leslie's eyes. "You said in your letter that some day I'd know why I had no business to buy the property for the site. Is today the day?"

"It may as well be." Peter Cairns looked away, his mind evidently engaged in choosing the words for his next utterance. "My name isn't Peter Cairns," he said deliberately. "It's Peter Carden. Alec Carden was my father. I ran away from him and his harsh tyranny. I changed my name to Cairns. The old Scotch name of our family was Cairrens. It became Carden in James the First's time."

"What?" Force of surprise brought out Leslie's habitual monosyllable. She wondered if she were awake or dreaming. Had her father, a lord of finance, once been a hot-headed rebellious boy who had changed his name and run away from Carden Hedge?

"Yes, what?" her father repeated half ironically. "My father left Carden Hedge to John, along with all he had. He disinherited me. When I went I took with me a bundle of bonds from the safe. They were mine; left me by my mother. I went to New York and made good. All this by the way of explaining about the garage site. You paid John Saxe sixty thousand dollars for a site that belonged to the Carden Estate. Not a foot of it belonged to the Saxe Estate. I had it surveyed and proved the Carden right to it. Saxe refunded the money. He was innocent in the matter."

Leslie's downcast reception of this last crushing surprise touched her father. "Buck up, Cairns II.," he said in the hearty, affectionate tone which Leslie had been dreading, yet longing, to hear. "I know I handed you a hummer. Now there's not much more to say, except that I bought Carden Hedge over two years ago of John. I've let him live there off and on, simply to have someone look after the property a little. I thought once of living there myself. I changed my mind. It's a pretty country up here. I liked it when I was a boy, and do still. I must be on my way tomorrow. How long would you like to stay in Hamilton?" He questioned with the old deference he had formerly observed to her wishes.

"I'd rather go back to New York with you." Leslie fought to keep her voice steady. "I can't. I want to stay on here a little and try to find a way to do something for the dormitory, or the college or the students—anything I can do to make up for—" She paused, regained composure, went on. "I'm to blame for keeping you out of happiness. I cheated myself, too. How could you care to live at the Hedge after what I did at Hamilton? I have learned the big lesson this time. I'd go back to college and begin all over again in spite of what might be said, if I could, Peter. I'd do it for you."

Peter Cairns saw a white-winged evanescent grace called happiness flit before his eyes. It had whisked away the day he had learned of Leslie's expulsion from college. "Perhaps we'll yet live at the Hedge, Leslie," he said. "We can do that much, if we can't go back in other ways. Now I'll make a bargain with you. If you can find any good and original reason for keeping your flivver I'll give the whole business to you as it stands. It must be original, though. That's the chief requirement. And it must be something that will benefit Hamilton College students, faculty, dormitory—in fact the whole aggregation. Go to it. You perfect the plan. I'll finance it for you. Nothing but the best will be accepted by me in the idea line. I'm going to try to prove that my girl has as good a brain as there is going."

CHAPTER XXIII.

A GREAT DAY FOR THE CAMPUS

Julia Peyton could have forgiven Doris Monroe for disagreeing with her. To be told by Doris that she was an object of dislike to the lovely sophomore was not to be borne. She held frequent indignant consultations with her roommate, Clara Carter, on the double subject of the ingratitude of Doris and the snippiness of Marjorie Dean. Julia had not forgiven Marjorie for her "interference" at the Rustic Romp.

Thus far she had not voiced the gossip on the campus that the foolish-faced farmer at the hop had been Leslie Cairns. She was a little afraid that such a bit of gossip on her part might bring down upon her Marjorie's displeasure. She knew in her heart that she was the only one of the four girls who would be likely to spread the story. Later on, when the Romp had been forgotten she would tell her friends about that horrid Miss Cairns and how she had stealthily slipped into the social side of Hamilton under cover.

Finding the desire to gossip irresistible she and Clara Carter entertained a soph with the tale one evening in their room. The soph, Lena Marsden, a quiet studious girl, had a flourishing crush on Doris. She promptly acquainted Doris with the ill news under promise of secrecy. "If some one like Miss Mason or Miss Harper, or any of the P. G.'s who have poise and influence would reprimand Miss Peyton, maybe she'd not talk about it any more." was Lena's opinion.

Leslie's repeated unkind and untruthful estimate of Marjorie had tended to destroy Doris's confidence in her, at least. Julia herself had spoken slightingly of Hamilton's most popular post graduate. Doris decided that of the seven post graduates she knew the two most likely to command the difficult silence of Julia were Veronica Lynne and Leila Harper. Her final choice fell upon Leila. She and Leila had grown quite friendly as the rehearsals of "The Knight of the Northern Sun" progressed. As her Norse lover, Godoran, Augusta Forbes and Doris had also progressed from stiff civility to real friendliness.

"Will you come to my room this afternoon about five, Miss Harper?" Doris requested on the day before that of a complete rehearsal of the play. In the act of leaving the dining room after luncheon Doris paused for an instant behind Leila's chair.

"With pleasure. I may be a little late, but I won't fail to come," Leila assured. Supposing Doris's request had something to do with the approaching rehearsal, Leila thought nothing further about it. It was twenty minutes past five that afternoon when she knocked on the door of Doris's room. It was the first time she had been asked to enter it by Doris. Muriel never entertained her chums there, "for fear of freezing them," she always said.

"There's something I must ask you, Miss Harper," Doris opened the conversation with an anxious little rush. She went on to lay the case of Julia's spite against Leslie before Leila. "I am sorry to have to mention Miss Cairns's name even to you. There seemed only this one way. I know I can trust you. I know you can suggest something."

Leila listened with laughter in her blue eyes. She had already been agitating her resourceful brain on the matter of Julia's garrulity. The plan she had dimly formed on the day when she and Marjorie had driven to Orchard Inn had developed better even than she had expected.

"I think I have a way of managing her," she said with a flashing smile of confidence.

"She is not easy to manage," warned Doris. "It will take something unusual to make an impression on her. She is envious and jealous and that blinds her to see much good in any one."

"I will see her when I leave you. I have seen Miss Cairns, Miss Monroe. Miss Dean and I met her on the way from Orchard Inn several days ago. She spoke to Miss Dean in my presence of the Romp. She is your friend, I believe, and is anxious that you shall not be blamed for anything. That is really all I wish to say in the matter." Leila gave Doris a straight, significant glance.

Doris settled back limply in her chair, "I—I—am surprised," she stammered. "I wish you—no, I don't, either. I'll ask Leslie. She will tell me what it's all about. I like Leslie, Miss Harper."

"I like her myself better than I used to," was Leila's careful answer.

"Have you—"

Doris did not finish. The door was flung open and a breezy, delighted shout of "Leila Greatheart!" ascended as Muriel Harding rushed upon Leila and hugged her. "Welcome to our cubicle! Why didn't you tell me you were coming to see me?"

"I cannot tell a lie. I didn't come here to see you at all, at all. I came to see Miss Monroe. Now I must be going. You may both come to see Midget and me this evening."

"Oh, I can't—that is—not this evening," Doris protested weakly. She dearly wished to accept the invitation.

"She means she won't come if I do," Muriel cheerfully supplied. Muriel's tone did not accord with her feelings. She was actually hurt, but gamely refused to show it.

"I meant nothing of the sort," Doris contradicted. Instantly she reflected that she had meant precisely that. "I beg your pardon," she addressed Muriel stiffly. "I did mean that. I don't now. I will come this evening, Miss Harper."

"Good night! I shall expect you both." Leila flashed out of the door, hurriedly closing it after her. Left to themselves the two girls might effect an understanding. She knew that Muriel was still vague as to why Doris had suddenly turned against her.

"Suppose we have it out this time, just to see how wrathful we can be," Muriel proposed, a shade of satire in the proposal. "That's the only way I know to break up a situation that's been hard on both of us. I've always thought the wires were crossed somewhere in Harding's and Monroe's last fight, but I couldn't prove it. Harding's and Monroe's last fight! Doesn't that sound thrilling? It makes one think of Indians, cowboys, rattlesnakes, buffaloes, prairies and—geese," she ended with a laugh.

"I hope it will be Harding's and Monroe's last fight," Doris said with sudden energy. "I know now that a certain other person was to blame for most of it. I know that you were not trying to be kind to me or belittle me. I'm not so sure about Miss Dean."

"She loves you, Doris Monroe." Muriel sprang into affectionate defense of Marjorie. "You never had a more faithful crush. She is the one who started the name of the fairy-tale princess for you. She has adored your beauty and wanted you to be in theatricals so that you could be seen and admired. She was the judge who delivered the adjuration to Beauty at the beauty contest. She is the best friend you have on the—"

Muriel stopped at sound of an odd little murmur from Doris. The fairy-tale princess had dropped into a chair with her golden head pillowed on one arm. Muriel's torrent of loving defense had fallen upon Doris like verbal hailstones. In fending for Marjorie she had forgotten her own side of the estrangement.

While the two were deep in amiable and verbose adjustment of their disagreement Leila was calling upon Julia Peyton. As she afterward confided to Vera: "I was there, Midget, with my tongue in my cheek."

Her interview with moon-eyed Julia appeared to be eminently satisfactory. She soon left the garrulous sophomore's room, followed by Julia to the door. Leila managed to walk down the hall to her own room after the interview with an air of dignity becoming to a post graduate. She was well aware that

Julia stood in the doorway of her room watching her. When she was safely within the walls of her own domicile she astonished Vera by making a laughing dive for her couch bed. She flung herself upon it and gave way to merriment.

"You should have been with me, Midget," she gasped. "I have had a lively time with the Screech Owl and the Phonograph. I have written a part for Miss Peyton in my new Irish play of 'Desmond O'Dowd.' It is that of Derina, the village gossip. She has not read it yet. When she does, I may have the part but no Screech Owl to play it. If you wish to tie your enemy's hands, offer him an honor. I have written the part of Derina especially to show this soph what she is. By the time she has rehearsed the part several dozen times she will wish to be any body but this one. I shall give her my personal attention. You know what that means. She may need a rehearsal every day. Hard on Leila. But think of the good to humanity!"

"Ingenious, you old star worshipper," laughed Vera. "Do you know she is, I believe, almost the only gossip on the campus. That's fine for Hamilton, isn't it? Every day we are growing better and better. Speaking of goodness reminds me of our own Marjorie. She and Jerry are coming over this evening."

"And I am expecting company; Matchless Muriel and the Ice Queen. Are they not a fine combination?" Leila cast a sly smile of triumph toward Vera. "How do you like my news, Midget?"

"I'm flabbergasted. Honestly, Leila, have those two patched up their quarrel?" Vera exhibited delighted wonder.

"Honestly, they have. Know, Midget, that I am always honest." She drew down a disapproving face. "How can you ask me such a question?" Immediately her engaging smile broke forth. "I have certainly a cheering budget of news for Beauty tonight. What with the thawing of the Ice Queen and the taming of the Screech Owl this has been a grander day on the campus than that of the Kerriberry Fair, in County Kerry, ould Ireland."

CHAPTER XXIV.

THE HAPPIEST PERSON

Easter vacation brought Captain Dean to Hamilton Arms and tumultuous happiness to Marjorie's heart. Greatly as she had come to love the Arms for its stately marvelous beauty and comfort, the loving devotion of Miss Susanna and the fact that it had been the home of Brooke Hamilton, she now loved it more strongly because it was graced by her adored captain's presence.

Since the morning when she had read the journal of Brooke Hamilton she had not written another word of his biography. "I can't write," she plaintively complained to Miss Susanna. "Spring and Captain and Brooke Hamilton's journal have all got into my brain and won't be shoved back. I'll have to get all over the strenuousness of them before I can go on writing."

"I think I shall lock up the study for a while, anyway," Miss Susanna threatened. "The Army owes a duty to its superior officer. I shall order Lieutenant Dean out on guide duty to Captain Dean. Ensign Hamilton and Corporal Macy will go along for company."

"*Corporal Macy.*" Jerry elevated her nose in deep disgust. "I'm a lieutenant myself. Kindly remember it. An ensign doesn't belong to the Army. An ensign belongs properly to the Navy."

"I shall be the great exception," persisted Miss Susanna, laughing. "Ensign sounds well with 'Hamilton.' It is not seemly for youth to scornfully contradict age."

"First show me age," retorted Jerry. "There ain't no such animal around here."

"I'm going to take Captain for a walk around the estate this morning," Marjorie announced. "There are oceans of things I want to show her and talk about. Almost every bush or tree at the Arms has an interesting history, all its own. Ensign Hamilton and, ahem, Corporal Macy are cordially invited to join the walk around."

"*Lieutenant* Macy doesn't regret that she has an engagement with Major Jonas Kent to plant dahlias this morning. Major Kent is far more polite than certain other officers of the detachment of far lesser rank," Jerry declined with significance.

"I ought to be, and I am, the happiest person in the world, I believe." Marjorie later voiced this fervent opinion as she sat on a rustic bench between her Captain and Miss Hamilton.

The three had seated themselves in the sweet spring sunlight at indolent ease after a long ramble about the magnificently kept grounds of the Arms. Under their feet the young green grass wove a soft living carpet. Over their heads spread the iron-strong branches of a mammoth tulip tree.

"Just because I am so happy, every once in a while I think of Mr. Brooke, Miss Susanna. Then I grow sad for a little. How beautiful it would have been for Angela and him to live here year after year in the perfect happiness of love! I often wonder how he had the courage to go through so many weary years after she left him. He chose such a patient, brave-hearted way."

"Perhaps he accomplished more of good because of such a sorrow than he might have wrought without it," sighed Miss Hamilton. "From the time of Angela's death he centered himself more than ever on the founding of Hamilton College. It might well be called a monument to the two women he loved. The nobility of plan and execution were inspired by his mother. But the beauty of nature which he cultivated and carried out with such rare taste and sentiment on the campus is his tribute to Angela. Day after day, early and late, he busied himself with enhancing the beauty of that overgrown grass plot. Perhaps his spirit communed with hers as he worked. This was before my time. You will find a packet of what he named, 'My garden letters,' among the data. If you haven't already been over it, you have a joy in store for you."

Miss Susanna stared absently out over the sea of living green splashed with the pale pinks, yellows and scarlets of early blooming shrubs. Mrs. Dean had taken no part in the conversation, preferring to listen. Marjorie's wistful observation regarding Brooke Hamilton and Angela Vernon had raised a feeling of surprise in her mind. It was the most sentimental word she had ever heard Marjorie utter.

Since her arrival at the Arms she had been permitted by Miss Hamilton to read the journal over which she had heard the Lady of the Arms and her lieutenant have several long discussions. Jerry had also been permitted to read it. She had at first cried over it, then impatiently characterized stately Brooke Hamilton as a "lovable old stupid" for not "getting it across" first thing that Angela was in love with him.

"I have a perfectly celostrous idea, children." Marjorie thus gaily designated the two beside her. "It came out of what you just said of Mr. Brooke and the campus." She lightly clasped Miss Susanna's arm. "I'll put Mr. Brooke's love idyl in 'Realization,' together with his nature work on the campus. That will do away with having to write of how he made Angela unhappy for so many years because he didn't know he loved her. I will state only that they met first when very young, and without knowing their own hearts. I think I will keep the entry about her riding down to the station with the picture to say good-bye to him." Marjorie turned to Miss Susanna, her eyes questioning.

"You are to do as you please, Marvelous Manager." Miss Susanna smiled into the beautiful, colorful face so near her own. "If you wished to publish the journal verbatim, I'd not gainsay you."

"I know you wouldn't, Goldendede." Marjorie returned the smile with interest. "I don't wish him to be misunderstood. He was not intentionally selfish. He was simply wrapped in his own great dream. The world, were it to read that journal, might call him hard-hearted. Even he reproached himself after he found that he loved Angela. I will leave out anything that I should not care to say of him myself. I pledged friendship with him in the beginning, you remember."

"I am glad you feel as I do about his love affair." Miss Susanna said with a grateful little nod. "I have always thought mention of it, at least, important in a biography of him. I was not sure what to do. I had thought, at the time when I talked with President Burns of having it prepared for publication, of submitting only a brief paragraph or two about Angela Vernon. I leave the matter contentedly to you."

"That's enough to bring back my lost inspiration," was the blithe declaration. "Come on, both of you." Marjorie sprang to her feet. She stretched an inviting hand to both her mother and Miss Susanna. "I shall proceed to hustle you about the rest of the grounds before luncheon. I'm going to the study to work this afternoon. Don't dare lock it up." She laid energetic command upon Miss Hamilton.

"What's to become of my sight-seeing tour?" doughtily demanded Miss Susanna.

"Corporal Macy will conduct it. Order her to it, and promise her a commission of major," Marjorie merrily proposed.

"Yes, genius is really beginning to burn again," Miss Susanna teasingly commented. "Jerry shall earn her commission." As she spoke she had allowed Marjorie to pull her to her feet.

"Let's walk down by the gate," Marjorie proposed. "I wish Captain to see that wonderful Chinese white lilac bush that once grew in the royal Chinese gardens."

They were not more than halfway across the space of lawn intervening between the rustic seat and the white, feathery plumed lilac bush when the eyes of all three picked up the trim lines of a small black roadster which had stopped at the entrance gates. There were two persons in the roadster. One of them, a tall, broad-shouldered man in gray tweeds and motor hat to match, was already out of the car. He had turned to give an assisting hand to a young woman who vaguely resembled him. She smiled happily at him as she stepped lightly to the ground. The two turned their backs on the car and approached the gates.

"It's Leslie Cairns!" Marjorie said in a low, astounded tone.

"It's—Can it be?" Miss Susanna shaded her eyes from the sun with a small, sturdy hand. "I believe it is—Peter Carden!"

CHAPTER XXV.

UNDER THE TULIP TREE

"Well, Peter, the years have dealt lightly with you," was Miss Susanna's greeting as she held out a hand to Alec Carden's runaway son.

She had heard from Marjorie of the recent agreeable change in Leslie Cairns. Marjorie had felt it only fair to Leslie to acquaint Miss Susanna with that change. The old lady now divined that Peter Carden had come to the Arms on a friendly errand. Her quick brain had instantly arrived at the truth as she glanced from Leslie to Peter Carden. Leslie was his daughter. Followed immediately the recollection of the financier's altered name.

"So you changed your name to Cairns, and this is your daughter," she continued with abruptness. In her astonishment she momentarily forgot to make introductions.

"Yes." Peter Cairns showed admiration of the intrepid little woman who had successfully fought off his bullying father and a college board largely composed of rascals. His keen eyes registered an expression of deference which he seldom accorded either men or women. "This is my daughter, Leslie, Miss Susanna." He drew Leslie gently forward. "She came to meet you and to see Miss Dean. I came to see you."

"I'm glad you have. I might not have said that years ago, but I can say it now." Miss Susanna introduced Peter Cairns and Leslie to Mrs. Dean, and the financier to Marjorie. The latter and Leslie had already exchanged friendly salutations.

Marjorie thought she had never before seen Leslie look so well. Beauty, even prettiness of the regulation type she would never have. There was a new expression of light and animation on her face, however, which made her what her father had often called her as a child: "his ugly beauty." The loose, unprepossessing droop to her mouth which Marjorie had formerly most disliked in her features was gone. A half humorous little quirk had taken the place of the ugly droop. It brightened her face wonderfully. Always of extremely symmetrical figure she was at her best today in a pale blue broadcloth dress. The softening grace of a wide summer fur draped her shoulders. Every detail of her apparently simple toilet had been carefully chosen. Leslie was a model of smart attiring.

"I don't feel much older than when I was Peter Harum-scarum, as John used to call me," smiled the financier. "I have had many a good and many a bad time at the Hedge. It has been mine for two years. I bought it from John. I am glad old Alec died. A hard thing to say of one's own father, perhaps. He had a hard hand, and a hard nature. I was glad to hear that you fought things to a finish with him."

"You may say what you please to me about Alec Carden, Peter. I know it will be the truth. I dislike to hear a man who was detested by his children while he lived hypocritically mourned by them after Providence has mercifully removed him from their midst," Miss Hamilton declared with candid relish. "Come up to the house and have luncheon with us. I hear you are a king of finance. Your history after you ran away from home must be interesting. You weren't more than twenty-four when you went, were you?"

"Twenty-five." Peter Cairns laughed, a short bitter sound. "Thank you for the invitation, Miss Hamilton. Some other day we'll accept with pleasure. We have a business engagement today with a man named Peter Graham." He and Leslie looked at each other and laughed.

Her glance toward him was a vivid brightening of feature which Marjorie thought beautiful. "Won't you come over and sit down under the big tulip tree?" she invited winningly. "We have been sitting there in the sunshine loving the spring outdoors."

"Yes, do. Peter, go and bring that seat over here under the tulip tree with the other," directed Miss Susanna pointing out a nearby rustic seat.

"Yes'm." The usually silent, taciturn man, who kept his large office force in a state of continual awe, ran like a boy to bring up the rustic bench and place it under the tulip tree opposite the other.

"Now, Peter, what in the world prompted you to come to see me?" the old lady inquired briskly, as she re-seated herself on the bench. Mrs. Dean courteously excused herself and walked on to the house. She decided that the four she had left would get along better without her. Miss Susanna and Leslie sat on one seat. Marjorie and Peter Cairns on the other.

"Oh, a number of things," Peter Cairns replied with an odd little duck of the head which Miss Susanna recalled him as a boy.

"You two," she indicated father and daughter, "are full of pleasant mystery. Your faces give you away."

"It is pleasant mystery; very pleasant," he replied with friendly conviction. "This is what it's all about." In his short-cut fashion he quickly outlined what he had already informed Leslie regarding the ownership of the site she had chosen on which to build the garage.

"I took the property away from Leslie because I was not pleased with her," he continued frankly. "Saxe refunded the money. He was entirely innocent in the matter. I took the sixty thousand dollars refund and invested it for Leslie. It was her money. She had paid far too much for the site. As the site belonged to the Carden estate and the Carden estate belonged to me I took over the whole garage enterprise. Leslie had to bear the loss of the money she had used for construction and other foolish purposes. I wanted to show her what a flivver she'd made.

"We agreed to tell this tale together. I've told my part of it. Now Leslie will tell hers. Your turn, Cairns II," he raised his heavy brows meaningly at Leslie.

"My father told me if I could think up a good reason for having my garage site back again, he would give it to me. The requirements were that whatever I wanted it for must benefit Hamilton College and all connected with it. He said it must be an original reason." Leslie came to the point with the same celerity as was Peter Cairns's habit.

"I tried at first to think of something that would work out with your plans, Miss Dean," she now addressed Marjorie. "I knew you had long since provided against emergency. Every time I thought of the word originality I thought of Leila Harper. I used to think when I was at Hamilton that she *was* originality." Leslie smiled briefly. "Miss Monroe raves over her. She says she is a dramatist, stage manager, actor and so forth. This is my idea. I'd like to build a theatre on the garage site. I'd call it the Leila Harper Playhouse. I'd present it to Hamilton College with the proviso that Miss Harper should always control the theatre and the policy of the plays. I would like to will her to Hamilton College as a rare dramatist, actor and manager." Leslie paused. Once fairly started on her proposal she had grown more and more animated.

"You take my breath!" Marjorie gave a little rapturous gasp. "I should say your plan was original. I think it's the very heart of gracious generosity. I love Leila, Miss Cairns, and wish more than I can say to have her appreciated and honored at Hamilton."

"She ought to be appreciated. She is going to be. You see a theatre will be of benefit to all the campus folks. It will be a source of amusement and pleasure to all. The money resulting from the plays should go to help the dormitory along. It will train girls who have histrionic ability for the stage. It will encourage students to play-writing. There will be prizes offered, so many each year for the best in plays, perhaps for exceptionally fine acting. My father will endow it. I shall put a part of my money into the endowment provided my idea is accepted by the Travelers. My name is not to be mentioned in it. My father doesn't wish his to be, either."

"None of the Travelers could or would refuse such an offer, Miss Cairns. Remember it is first of all for Leila. She has worked so hard to give the campus good plays. Not to mention all the splendid things she's done for

Hamilton as a Traveler." Marjorie sang Leila's praises with a high heart. "Yet none of us would wish yours or your father's name to be withheld. It would be our grateful pleasure to tell others of your splendid gift."

"You make it seem the thing for us to do—I don't know. Let me come again and talk with you about it. My father and I are partners now," she threw him a fond comradely glance. He and Miss Susanna had listened and let youth talk out its own matters of interest.

It was an hour later when Peter Cairns and Leslie left the Arms, happy in the long step that had been taken that day toward the partnership of which they had talked and dreamed in bygone years in New York.

"Miss Susanna has changed more than any other person I ever knew," were the financier's first words to Leslie as they drove away from Hamilton Arms. "She was a sweet woman until after she had so much trouble with my father and that rascally board. I was only a little boy then. I never saw her again after I left Carden Hedge until a few years ago when I came up here to see John. She looked like a fierce, sullen little creature of the wild, ready to snarl at a word. Now she is charming. She looks as though she had found what we have—happiness."

"Blame it on Bean," Leslie said with a shadow of her old satiric smile. "She can change anything. She even put over the great transformation on me."

Back at the Arms Jerry, who had successfully put dozens of plump dahlia tubers into the soft brown earth under Jonas's somewhat critical eye, was now racing across the lawn to the tulip tree.

"I saw the company from afar. Who were they?" she called out when within a few feet of the rustic benches where Miss Susanna and Marjorie had reseated themselves. "No one I ever saw before. I couldn't label either one of them."

"You have seen them both before, Jeremiah," Marjorie calmly assured. "The young lady was Leslie Cairns. The man was—our gasoline bogie."

"What-t? Has one hob-goblin wed another. Don't tell me the grand Hob-goblin is married!" Jerry looked ridiculous consternation.

"Who said anything about being married. The gasoline bogie is Leslie Cairns's father."

"Then he must be a house robber. What was he doing around the Carden estate at that hour of the night?" Jerry demanded.

"He is not a house robber." Marjorie was now laughing. "He is a house owner. He owns Carden Hedge, and his name is Peter Carden. He is the Carden son who ran away from home and changed his name to Peter Cairns.

"Good night." Her eyes on Marjorie, Jerry went to sit down on the end of one of the two benches. She missed the bench and sat down forcefully on the soft grass.

"Can you beat it?" she giggled as she scrambled to her feet and dropped down beside Marjorie, this time in the middle of the bench. "Can you blame me for that flivver? I've heard of being overcome by astonishment. It just happened to Jeremiah."

CHAPTER XXVI.

THE IRISH MINUET

The Travelers presented "The Knight of the Northern Sun" at the Hamilton Concert Hall on the evening after that of the re-opening day of college following the Easter vacation. Lucy Warner had asked and received President Matthews's hearty permission to use the hall for the Norse play and afterwards for any other attractions which Page and Dean might wish to offer.

The Norse play was the most ambitious drama the Travelers had yet undertaken. They had gone to great trouble and pains to costume and produce the play inexpensively, but with realism. Nor was the audience which crowded the large hall to the doors composed entirely of students. Since the presentation of the first show by Page and Dean almost two years previous, interested citizens of the town of Hamilton and residents of Hamilton Estates had shown flattering eagerness to obtain seats for Page and Dean's shows.

Augusta Forbes scored heavily as Godoran, the Norse hero, who, until he met the fair Nageda, boasted that he had looked earnestly at no woman's face save his mother's. Doris was the lovely, golden-haired Nageda, who fell in love with Godoran at sight but was carried off as a hostage by barbarian hordes on the day of her initial meeting with her hero.

The play netted the dormitory fund over a thousand dollars. Augusta and Doris stepped into the spot light of campus admiration and were fêted by their friends for upwards of a week afterward. Marjorie attended the presentation of the drama with her mother, Jerry, Miss Susanna and Jonas. It was her mother's last evening at the Arms and this sad knowledge put her in a rather forlorn mood. Then, too, she could not help thinking of Hal. She had suggested the title of the play as a result of seeing the costume of polar knight Hal Macy had worn at the merry-making in Sanford on Christmas Eve. Now she saw Hal as the knight, rather than Gussie.

She wondered vexedly why she always thought of Hal in connection with the sentimental. It was because he had told her he loved her, she supposed. She watched fascinatedly the progress of the play and listened with half impatient sadness to the impassioned words of love which Katherine Langly, who knew nothing about love, had put into the mouth of Godoran.

Following the play and her mother's departure for Sanford, Marjorie returned with conscientious interest to the work of the biography. Since the love story of Brooke Hamilton had entered into it she had revolutionized her whole idea of the plan. Now she plunged once more into the journal, working at it diligently. She tried to use every sentence of it which did not touch too personally on the side of the great man's romance which belonged to him and not to the world.

After a time it seemed to her that she knew every line of the journal by heart. She worked steadily on through the bright spring weather until she had arranged the delicate matter to suit her critical mind. Miss Susanna was greatly pleased over Marjorie's arranging of the sentimental part of her great-uncle's history. She had taken a notion to edit the garden letters herself, and the two friends worked together in the study at the long library table, each with the same fond spirit toward the man in the portrait.

On the campus Leila Harper in fancy had ceased to be a post graduate. Instead she was living through an exciting period of Irish history as she rehearsed the heroic part of Desmond O'Dowd. As the time drew near for the presentation of the Irish drama she grew more pleased with the work of the cast than she had ever been with that of any other group of actors whom she had formerly used in her plays. Vera, as Mona of Lough Gur, the Irish maid from County Limerick, promised to be the chief attraction.

One thing to perfect her production Leila lacked. She needed a real man, one with an exceptionally sweet tenor voice to sing words to the minuet tune that accompanied the Irish minuet she and Vera were to give in the first act of the play. As the hero it was really Leila's place to sing the quaint words as she danced. Not being possessed of a tenor voice she could not carry out this part of the program. She decided after much thought to place a singer in the wings to voice the pretty Irish words.

Next difficulty was to obtain the singer. Following a brief season of despairing calculation as to whether a church singer in Hamilton might not undertake the solo, Leila hit upon another plan that brought a true Cheshire cat grin to her keen Celtic features. She hastily mailed a very ragged piece of Irish music to Hal Macy with a short accompanying letter, and buoyantly awaited results.

Leila's plan to bring Hal from Sanford to sing behind the scenes for her on the night of her play was not entirely one of self-interest. She had often thought Marjorie was nothing less than a sleeping beauty slated to awaken suddenly from a dream of life to reality and a lover's kiss. She had long guessed for herself that Hal loved Marjorie. She had also been the only one besides Marjorie who had seen Hal's heart-broken expression as he had stood before Marjorie's portrait.

Of late Leila had shrewdly thought she had noticed signs of absent-minded dreaming on Marjorie's part which might or might not have to do with Hal.

Miss Susanna had decreed that Marjorie might tell the original Travelers of the journal if she wished. Leila had listened to Marjorie's sad account of it and her wistful remarks afterward with her head on one side. She had there and then made up her mind to try out an experiment of her own upon Hal and Marjorie.

In due time Hal's answer returned. Yes, he would be pleased to help her with her play in any way he could. He would make it a point to keep out of sight until after the performance. This Leila had also requested. He had learned the Irish song and thought it very pretty. Leila was tempted more than once to tell Jerry. She triumphantly fought off the desire and cannily kept her own counsel.

Now wholly engaged in what promised to completely outdo "The Knight of the Northern Sun," Leila paid little attention to anything else. As she worked steadily and patiently toward perfecting the various actors in the difficult Celtic characters they were to represent she did not dream that she had already been selected as an object for honor.

Leslie Cairns had determined that Leila should receive her gift, and her father's, of a theatre on the last day of chapel. Leslie had always remembered and been impressed by the various honor citations which she had witnessed when a student at Hamilton. She believed that Leila would prefer to be honored in the company of her fellow students in chapel than at the regular Commencement exercises. She argued that the gift she wished to offer Leila was germane to the traditional side of the college.

While Leila was carrying on a lively correspondence with Hal, Marjorie was wondering now and then why she had not heard from him. With Hal so much in her mind of late it was not strange that she should notice his delay in writing. She had written him over a month ago. He had not written to Jerry, either. Perhaps he had been away, or had been ill. No; if he had been ill Jerry's mother would have mentioned it to Jerry in a letter. Marjorie realized, all of a sudden, that she had grown quite concerned in the matter. She chided herself for being silly, and dismissed Hal from her thoughts—until he happened to walk into them again.

"Say, have you heard from old Hal lately?" Jerry asked her on the evening of Leila's play, as the two girls were dressing for the event. "Because I'm going to wear my turquoise necklace I happened to think of him. He gave it to me, you know."

"I've wondered myself why he hasn't answered my last letter." Marjorie stood before the long wall mirror surveying herself with a critical and unenthusiastic eye. She was dressed in the shaded violet frock of Chinese crepe which she had owned for five years and which was still a la mode. She had worn it only on rare occasions. It was still fresh and charming as on the night when she had worn it as a freshman to the Beauty contest. Leila had begged her to wear it "in honor of your Celtic friend and Irish playwright," she had laughingly stipulated.

"He's probably away on a business trip for the governor." Jerry delivered this opinion as she poked her arms into her white fur evening coat. "Don't forget your violets." She patted the huge bunch of scented purple beauties at her own corsage.

Marjorie turned from the mirror. She took her own bunch of violets from the water, dried the stems and pinned them on. The faint exquisite perfume of them all but brought tears to her eyes. She thought of Angela, of Brooke Hamilton, of how they had loved violets. And then—back went her mind to the winter day when Hal had stood before the portrait of a girl who wore violets.

"I'm going for a long, long walk tomorrow," she announced. "My head is full of cobwebs. I shall let the fresh air sweep it clear. I hope there will be a good old high wind blowing. I'll love to walk out and fight with it."

"I'll go with you. Bean. Never believe you can lose me."

"I look upon you as a permanent fixture," Marjorie graciously assured.

"Make the most of me tonight. I'm going to leave you tomorrow. I happen to remember that I can't be always with you." Jerry trailed out the remark in a melancholy tone. "I like the permanent fixture idea, but I can't be it. I have to go the round of the campus houses tomorrow and see what I can gather up for the auction. There are times when I wish I were not quite so necessary to Hamilton," was Jerry's regretfully modest ending.

"You don't know what you are talking about." Marjorie gave a funny little chuckle. "First you said I couldn't lose you. Then you said just the opposite."

"I know it. I seem to be like that, don't I?" Jerry beamed foolishly upon her lovely chum.

Marjorie got into her own evening coat, a springtime affair of pale tinted silk and lace, and the pair paraded downstairs arm in arm. Jerry's nonsense had served to restore Marjorie's lighter spirits to normal light-heartedness. During the short ride in the limousine to Hamilton Concert Hall an energetic conversation occupied the attention of all three. It concerned the library which was to be presented to the dormitory girls when the dormitory should be completed.

Miss Susanna was determined that the students who were now the dormitory seniors should be present the next fall when the dormitory would be finished and opened. She had just announced her intention of defraying the railway expenses of the graduate "dorms" wherever they might be.

All three were also happy over Guiseppe Baretti's present to the dormitory. He had long announced his intention of giving the "dorm a nice present." A few days previous he had sent for Robin and Marjorie and solemnly informed them that he wished to take the expense of furnishing the dorm with the best grill room that money could secure. "I buy all for it; all," he declared with an inclusive spread of the arms. "Then I do this. What you want buy. You give me the list ev'ry week. I buy for the dorm same I buy for me. This don' cost me half's much it cost the dorm." His offer was accepted with the same deep gratitude which it seemed to Marjorie that the Travelers owed almost everyone.

The orchestra pit of the hall looked like a florist's shop. As the trio entered the fragrance of roses and violets was wafted to their nostrils.

"Um-m. All the actors are in line for a donation," muttered Jerry. "I hope our offerings to the bunch haven't been side tracked." The Travelers had gathered up among themselves a goodly sum of money for the purpose of honoring the members of the cast with flowers. Vera's dainty pen and ink were all gone before the Hamilton Arms detail reached there.

"Miss Mason said to tell you that she had saved some sketches for you," was the comforting assurance that met the party at the door. The message was delivered by a sophomore who was doing usher duty.

Seats of honor well up front had been reserved for the mistress of the Arms and her bodyguard. Seated in the brilliantly lighted room, the perfume of flowers on the air, the pleasant, well-bred murmur of subdued voices in her ears Marjorie thrilled to it all as she had always vibrated to the social side of Hamilton College.

She loved to think of herself as a part of it, alive and moving along with that busy, mind-profitable life. She was glad that she had such clever, wonderful friends. Not one of her chums but that had specialized in some particular talent or craft. She alone was the only one who had no hold on the fine arts beyond being an appreciative worshipper of those who were talented. Thus her thoughts ran until the rise of the curtain on "Desmond O'Dowd."

From then on she thought only of the play itself. Leila herself had arranged the most of the setting for the first act. The opening scene was laid in the old-fashioned hall of an Irish country house of early eighteenth century. Desmond O'Dowd, the hero, whose free thinking and free speech had placed him in disfavor with the Earl of Claflin, had come to Claflin Eyrie, the earl's home, in the hope of seeing Mona, the earl's niece. He wished to say goodbye to her before joining a revolutionary political party which he believed to be the only one working for the good of Ireland.

It was during this act that Leila and Vera were to dance the Irish minuet of which the Hamilton girls were so fond. The play opened with a number of young men and women of Mona's acquaintance gathered for a little evening party. The high-waisted, comparatively simple costumes of the young women were dainty foils for the dark knee trousers, square cut coats, silk stockings, fancy low shoes and lace falls of the young men. Shoulder length hair, ribbon-tied, formed a part of the picturesque dressing of the young Irish gentlemen of this period.

After a gay little dance in which the whole company joined, came the entrance into the hall of Desmond. Leila played the part with true Celtic intensity and understanding. Vera who took color from constant association with Leila, was no less convincing in the role of dainty Mona. Marjorie leaned forward in her seat breathlessly waiting for the moment to come which would introduce the minuet. She had seen it danced by the two a number of times and never tired of it. She was particularly fond of the charming setting of words that went with a part of the tune. The minuet had special music which Leila had brought from Ireland and which was very old.

"Leila can't sing the words this time," Marjorie whispered to Jerry. "She was grumbling to me about it not so very long ago. She can't sing like a man and she doesn't care to sing them in her own voice."

The pleading, persuasive voice of Desmond to Mona, saying: "Just one dance, acushla. Tomorrow I'll be far away across the lakes and with only the thought of you and your love to keep my poor heart from breaking."

Marjorie breathed a long sigh of anticipatory pleasure as the preliminary strains of the minuet rose from the orchestra pit where Phillys Moore was conducting her own capable ten piece orchestra. With the usual number of deep, courtly bows the minuet began. Followed the gradual advance down the center of the pair of dancers. The odd, dainty stepping, dignified in its deliberateness. Each step in perfect accord with each note of the music combined to make a poetry of motion difficult to describe. Then—From somewhere off stage a voice suddenly began to sing:

"Down the center little one,

Life for us has just begun:

Down the center, step together,

Only you and I are one forever.

Colin he is watching me,

His love you can never be,

Step together, part we never

Sweetheart wee."

It was a high, sweet tenor voice, vigorous of tone yet giving the Irish lilt the true lyric delicacy necessary to the rendering of any Irish song. Marjorie listened to it, entranced, yet with the vague impression that she had heard it somewhere before.

"Forward, forward,

Higher, sweeter, sounds the measure,

You for me, my small white treasure

You for me, for now and aye, love."

The voice sang on, seeming to grow more and more impassioned. The tender import of the love words brought a quick veil of tears to Marjorie's eyes. It was all so real. The two lovers, surrounded in the very beginning with unsurmountable difficulties, their brave attempt to defy life and fate. Ardent Desmond pleading for the constancy of his "small white treasure." Then that voice, ringing, a thread of defiant laughter running through its music.

Marjorie came back to reality in time to hear an excited voice in her ear growling softly: "Old Hal. Now can you beat that. It is Hal that's doing the singing. I know it. That's some of Leila Harper's work. Oh-h-h. Wait until I grab both of them. I'm going behind the scenes the minute the show's over. I'd go at the end of the first act, but I might make a nuisance of myself. If Hal Macy knows what is good for him he will march himself out front like a kind and loving brother."

Marjorie heard Jerry's words in a kind of pleased daze. She was conscious of one emotion above everything else. She would be very glad to see Hal. She wished he would soon come to them. But Hal did not appear. Wily Leila had enlisted his services in helping with a mob scene at the end of the second act. She needed him again to direct another third-act ensemble where the revolutionists gather about their chief, Desmond O'Dowd, in the haunted house at the foot of the Cragsmore cliff. Leila knew precisely what she was about in keeping Hal from Marjorie. She was certain both Jerry and Marjorie must have recognized his singing voice.

When the final curtain had descended after Leila and the cast had been surfeited with flowers and curtain calls, and after Leila had made a speech of few and embarrassed words, Hal had still not appeared.

"Let him go." Jerry had grown out of patience. "I disown him. I never had a brother. I'll will old Hal to Leila Harper for a stage hand. She has kept him back on the stage and made him work. She—" Jerry suddenly subsided with an articulate murmur.

Marjorie looked blank. She had never before thought of Leila Harper in conjunction with Hal. How had Hal happened to know the words to the old Irish song? Leila must have sent them to him by letter. No, she must have sent the music for the minuet. She thought that he had not been in Hamilton more than a few hours. Still he might have been on the campus all day and she had never—

There she stopped. Leila was her most devoted friend. She was glad that Hal had at last shown a preference for some one beside herself. Marjorie stopped the thought process again. She found she did not wish to think about Hal and Leila as being interested in each other. She wondered next if they had been corresponding long. Leila had never mentioned in her presence that she had received a letter from Hal. Leila had—

"Marjorie." The sound of the voice whose tender cadences had lately thrilled her was now speaking her name, and in the same ardent tone.

"Oh, Hal." Involuntarily both hands went out to meet the strong warm ones which clasped her slender fingers close.

"You gave us a positive electric shock," complained Jerry. "How long have you been here? Give an account of yourself."

"Not very long." Hal relinquished Marjorie's hands slowly, deliberately. She stood looking at him with an expression of sweet welcome which came to him vaguely as something he had not hitherto seen in her face.

He had already warmly greeted Miss Susanna. She was now engaged in conversation with Professor Wenderblatt, who had come up to speak to her.

"There's Lillian Wenderblatt over by the orchestra pit talking to Phil. I must see her about the auction. Back in a minute." Jerry had not noticed any difference in Marjorie's demeanor toward Hal. She left the two together on general principles.

"Were you surprised to hear my voice before you saw me?" Hal asked with a smile. He was trying to tell himself that he must not show Marjorie that he loved her. She did not like that.

"Yes; I didn't recognize it for a minute. I only knew it was familiar—and beautiful," she added with her charming lighting up of feature.

"Thank you. How are you, Marjorie, and the biography? You are the portrait girl tonight, aren't you?" Hal was struggling valiantly to be impersonal. He wished instead to say to this lovely violet girl: "I love you. I love you." The grace of her beauty was in his heart. The perfume from the violets at her waist was a breath of sweetness to his hungry soul.

"Yes, I am wearing my violet dress. I am well. The biography is progressing very slowly." Marjorie felt an odd little chill at Hal's pleasant inquiries.

"I'm going to the Arms with you," Hal announced. "Miss Susanna insists that I shall stay there tonight. I must be on my way tomorrow. I'm planning a trip to Alaska. Expect to be gone all summer. I'll go over to the campus tomorrow before I leave and call on Leila. She certainly is a grand old comrade."

"I love Leila Greatheart, Hal," Marjorie said loyally. "I'm so glad you came here to help her with her play."

"Aren't you just a little bit glad to see me for myself, Marjorie?" Hal could not resist putting this one question.

"You know I am." Marjorie attempted to look into his face with her old-time frank smile. She smiled, but the smile was one of shyness. Her brown eyes rested on Hal only an instant. The rose deepened in her cheeks. Hal looked at her, and wondered.

CHAPTER XXVII.

ROMANCE

"The magic of yon sailing moon

Lures my poor heartstrings out of me;

God's moonshine whitens the lagoon:

The earth's a silver mystery."

"Why, Hal, I didn't know you knew that poem!" Marjorie stood beside Hal at the top of the veranda steps bathed in the white moonlight. Looking at her, Hal had quoted the verse of old Irish poetry. "Leila must have taught you that." She smiled, but there was a tiny ache in her heart.

"*You* taught me that. You recited it one night when we were down on the beach. That was last summer. It seems longer ago."

"So I did. I had forgotten." For some unknown reason Marjorie felt lighter of heart. The tiny pain was gone.

"That was a white moonlight night. So is this. Come and take a walk." Hal stretched out a hand to Marjorie.

"Just a little way." She followed him down the steps, but laughingly refused his hand. "I know this place better than you. I don't need a guide," she said. "We mustn't go far from the veranda. I am hungry. We are soon going to have a midnight supper, especially for you."

"I'm grateful for hospitality. What a corking old piece of magnificence the Arms is! I wish I had time to see it thoroughly. I'd invade your study and bother you. I give you fair warning."

"Why can't you stay at the Arms for a few days, Hal? Jerry will be so disappointed. You can't know as I know how much she loves you."

"I know." Hal nodded. "Jerry will be home before long. But you won't be home for—" He paused. "Are you coming home in June?"

"I don't know." The answer came doubtfully. "The biography won't be finished until some time next winter. I must come back to Hamilton next fall to see to our dormitory interest. There are other things, too. Captain and General wish me at home, and Miss Susanna wishes me here, and—

"I want you myself, Marjorie." Hal's quick utterance had the virile quality now which had thrilled her when he sang. "Why do I tell you this again when

I've sworn to myself I'd never trouble you? I don't know. I only know that you seem to me tonight to be—kinder."

"Hal, I—" They were crossing the lawn now strolling aimlessly along under the moon's pale rays. They came to an immense flowering almond bush. It lifted burgeoning pink clusters, a mass of rioting bloom under the white light.

"Hal, I always mean to be kind to you." Marjorie did better this time. "I wish you wouldn't feel that you have troubled me. I have read Brooke Hamilton's love story. I understand more of love than I used. I know that true love is—it is—"

"What do you know of love?" Hal's hands suddenly dropped lightly upon her shoulders. The two had stopped before the great pink bush, facing each other, their young features set with the terrific earnestness of youth. "Have you grown up? Do you love me?"

"I—have grown up this much—I—understand the worth of true love, Hal. That is—"

"Not loving me yet, but very near it," came the tender interruption. Hal's hands slipped from Marjorie's shoulders. "I love you," he said. "I love you."

Marjorie regarded him silently. She knew that Hal was fighting against loving her. That in a moment of emotion he had spoken again the words he had tried to forget. He would instantly go back to his role of devoted friend. She did not wish him to go back. She loved him. How greatly she loved him she could not then guess. She knew only that she loved him.

"What is it, Marjorie?" Hal reached for her hands, caught them, held them unresisting in his own.

Came a silence. A faint vagrant night breeze stirred the trees, touched the faces of the two besides the almond bush. Very gently Hal drew his Violet Girl into his arms.

"It must be a whole year from now, Hal," Marjorie said later with charming practicality. They were walking toward the house now in answer to at least five minutes' intermittent whistling of Jerry from the veranda.

"Stop a minute." Hal drew Marjorie into the shadow of a tall shrub.

"I have oceans to do. I told you all about it a little while ago. Work is work. It can't be done in a minute. But it can be accomplished by next June. Then I'll be—I'll be—"

"Marjorie Dean Macy," Hal said, and he punctuated these three euphonic words in true lover's fashion. The story of that eventful year of accomplishment and triumph, which ended in the dawn of a perfect wedding day for Marjorie, will be told in: "MARJORIE DEAN MACY."

THE END.

Lightning Source UK Ltd.
Milton Keynes UK
UKHW010745271222
414464UK00004B/294

9 789356 785830